# Vampire Journal

# Vampire Journal

**Don Conroy**

Published 1997
by Poolbeg Press Ltd
123 Baldoyle Industrial Estate
Dublin 13, Ireland
E-mail: poolbeg@iol.ie
www.poolbeg.com



Reprinted October 2000



A catalogue record for this book is available from the British Library.

ISBN 1 85371 871 8



Cover design by Steven Hope
Illustrations by Don Conroy
Set by Poolbeg Group Services in Goudy 11.5/16
Printed by The Guernsey Press Ltd,
Vale, Guernsey, Channel Islands.

## *About the Author*

Don Conroy is a well-known writer of children's fiction, television personality and an enthusiastic observer of wildlife. He sketches animals and birds native to Ireland and is one of Ireland's best-loved writers and illustrators for children.

For Sarah

# Chapter One

"It's not Jerakala," snapped Vinny. "The name is Dracula."

"Sorry about that," said his pal, Peter.

Vinny looked at Julie and Gary then, with an obvious gesture of his head, threw his eyes up to heaven. "It's important to be precise, you know what I mean. Otherwise people won't take you serious."

"Seriously," said Julie.

"Oh yeah, seriously," quipped Vinny, as he emptied the last drop from his can of Pepsi Max.

"This is a deadly poster," Julie, who had carefully opened it out, remarked.

"Oh yeah, *The Skull* . . . now that was a great movie. It had Peter Cushing and Christopher Lee in it."

"Peter Cushing . . . I know that name . . . wasn't he in *Star Wars?*"

"Yes," said Vinny. "But he's best known for films like *Dracula*, *Frankenstein*, *The Mummy*, and *The Gorgon*."

"It must have been deadly making films like that," remarked Peter.

"Scary, I would say," said Julie.

"According to my Uncle Tommy, Christopher Lee doesn't like the term *horror* films. Horror is something like people dying in an earthquake or a fire."

"Or being shot in the head," added Peter.

"Yeah . . . real life stuff that is gruesome."

"Yes, I see what he means," said Julie. "Creepy films are more about mystery and imagination."

"That's it, Julie, spot on. Now, most people are into the modern horror movies. But Uncle Tommy says they're all just blood and guts, no imagination at all."

"The special effects are good," said Gary.

"Well, they'd have to be, since the stories are brutal," said Vinny.

"My parents would never get out a horror film on video. My dad thinks they're all rubbish. He likes anything with sport in it. My ma loves something with romance, you can't beat a good love story, she always says," said Peter.

"Well, let's not go off at a tangent," said Vinny. "We met today to start a horror club!"

"I've brought a book I got in the local bookshop," said Julie. "It cost me two pounds; it's second-hand but it's in fairly good nick." She handed it to Vinny.

Vinny fingered the book. "*Vampire Omnibus*. That's brill. There's alot of stories in it."

Julie was pleased that Vinny liked her contribution to the club.

"That's very good value," said Gary. "You'd pay about a tenner for that if you were to buy it new."

"Well, as you can see, it must have got damp or wet and that's the reason I got it so cheap."

"Anybody else manage to bring anything?" asked Vinny.

"I brought some things," said Gary. "I hope you don't think they're stupid." He put his hand into his jacket pocket and produced a brown bag. It looked like a sweet bag. All eyes watched the bag as Gary slowly put it down on the bed. He then placed his hands on the bag like he was about to perform a magic trick. With his hands either side of the brown bag he gently pulled it open. Then he put one hand carefully into the opening and withdrew a small plastic bottle.

"What's that?" Peter asked.

Gary screwed off the cap, put his index finger on the top, quickly upended it and returned it to the upright position. He then displayed his finger. "Look," he said proudly. "Blood!" They all laughed. "It's the stuff they use in the movies and on stage." A little disappointed by their response, Gary said eagerly, "I've more." He pulled from the bag four sets of plastic vampire teeth. "One for each of us."

They picked them up and popped them into their mouths over their own teeth, closed their mouths and, as they did, their lips parted, revealing evil grins. They hurried over to the mirror in Vinny's bedroom and began to grin and growl at their own reflections. They broke into loud shouts and screams, pulling all kinds of ghoulish faces.

Suddenly the bedroom door was pushed open. Vinny's big sister Amanda stood there in her dressing-gown. "Will you all keep quiet! I'm trying to get some sleep."

"Sorry," said Vinny. "We were only messing." He tried to talk with the teeth in.

They removed them a little sheepishly. Amanda gave them all a hard stare. "Be a bit considerate of other people who are trying to sleep . . . creeps!" She turned on her heel and went back to her own room.

"Don't mind her, she's always like a demon if someone wakes her."

"It's twelve o'clock," said Peter.

"I know," said Vinny. "But she works late in the supermarket on a Friday, then she goes to a disco or club and she's not in until all hours . . . What are we talking about my big sister for, anyway? So far we have a few good posters and some excellent film stills, a couple of books and some props," he said, opening and closing the plastic fangs with his fingers.

"I brought something," said Peter. He was holding a plastic bag from a bookshop. "No one will ever guess what it is," he said with confidence.

"It's a book," said Gary, reading the writing on the bag.

Peter shook his head.

"Is it a video?" asked Julie. "Come on, Peter, don't keep us all in suspense."

Peter pulled out a crucifix. "Back, fiends! Back!"

They laughed loudly. "Shush! We don't want the dragon back," said Vinny.

Julie examined the cross. "That's beautiful. It's brass, isn't it?"

"Yes, it belonged to my aunt, she was a nun. It was one of the things given to us in her will. It used to be on the wall in the hallway of our house. My dad took it down when he wallpapered the place. It never went back up."

Vinny took the cross. "It's quite heavy. This would be very handy if we came across a real vampire." They all laughed. "Listen, you'd all better go . . . I'll meet you in Herbert Park at two o'clock."

"Where?" asked Peter.

"Just below the steps, on a bench you know, beside the duck pond."

"Oh yeah," said Peter. "Glad you mentioned the pond. There's a lot of benches in the park."

"I did say below the steps," snapped Vinny. "Use your noggin."

"What's happening in the afternoon?" asked Julie.

"Well, my uncle Tommy . . . listen, I'll save it for later . . . keep you all in suspense."

"Stop all the thumping," snapped Vinny's father as they hurried down the stairs.

"Sorry, Mr Quinn," said Julie as she opened the hall door.

"See you later," said Gary, slipping past Mr Quinn then out the door.

"Oh, I forgot my bag," said Peter, running back up the stairs.

"Your poor sister is trying to sleep." Vinny's father prodded him with his index finger.

Vinny's mother came in from the kitchen. "That girl should be up by now. Amanda! Amanda! are you going to stay in bed all day? Get up now."

"I'm getting up," shrieked a voice from upstairs.

Peter came charging down the stairs. "Oh hello, Miss Quinn . . . Mrs Quinn, I mean. Hello, Mr Quinn. See you later, Vinny. Two o'clock on the dot."

"See you," said Vinny, closing the door.

"Before you think of going anywhere you better cut the grass, and tidy up all those videos. I nearly walked on one this morning."

"Yes, Da." Vinny smiled. "By the way, Da . . ." Vinny nodded his head trying to indicate something.

"What?" enquired his father.

"My pocket money?"

"Please," said his mother.

"Please," said Vinny in parrot-fashion.

His father scowled and plunged his hands deep into the pockets of his bus driver's trousers. "There." He placed five pound coins in his palm. "When I was thirteen, I was lucky to get a shilling."

"Say thanks," said his mother, clipping him over the head in a friendly fashion.

"Thanks, Da!"

"Where are you off to in the afternoon?"

"I'm off to see Uncle Tommy, Ma."

"Bring him over a rhubarb tart and tell him we'll expect him for lunch tomorrow."

"You pamper that brother of mine," Vinny's father said gruffly.

"Listen, Paddy, you know he hasn't been too well lately with his chest."

"He should give up that bloody pipe or at least buy decent tobacco. I'm convinced he smokes peat."

"You should talk . . . you used to smoke those dreadful coffin nails."

"That was nearly three years ago," he snapped.

"Three . . . and another forty years," she teased.

"Well, I'm off them three years next month, and I don't miss them."

"What's for lunch, Ma?" asked Vinny.

"Spaghetti bolognese. It'll be ready in a few minutes. Time enough for you to cut the grass, put away your tapes and wash your hands."

"Here, before you do that . . ." said his father. "Slip around and get a block of ripple ice cream for your mother's apple tart. Here's a fiver, and bring back the paper, and the change!"

When Vinny arrived in the park he found his friends already waiting for him on the bench.

"What's in the bag?" asked Gary.

"It's a rhubarb tart for my uncle."

"You missed it," said Peter. "It was deadly."

"What was deadly?" asked Vinny.

"We just saw a hawk, a sparrow-hawk, right over there." He pointed at the bushes near the pond.

"Yeah, we were just sitting here when we noticed a flock of sparrows feeding on the ground."

"They were having a dust-bath," interrupted Peter showing off his knowledge.

"Well, whatever they were doing," Julie continued, "we noticed a large bird passing over the top of the bushes. We knew it wasn't a crow. It suddenly darted down after the flock. They all scattered."

"It didn't catch any," said Gary, "but it was a deadly chase."

"I'd love to have seen that," sighed Vinny. "If it hadn't been for Amanda asking me to call over to Chrissie Doyle with a message I would have been here and would have seen it."

"Well, if we saw it today," said Julie, 'the chances are it lives around here and could come again another day."

"Perhaps you're right," said Vinny stoically.

"Of course, they are rather secretive," Peter added. "Hawks."

"You're a quare hawk! Let's go," said Vinny. "We'll go down by the Dodder river."

They passed up a side trail from the pond and across the football pitches until they reached the small gate that leads out on to the Dodder walkway. They saw a moorhen on the water and some mallard that flew in from the park.

"I've seen kingfishers here," said Vinny proudly. "And a dipper," indicating to the others that he knew as much about wildlife as Peter. "You know, when I was very small my da would bring me to visit my uncle and we always would buy a few chocolate éclairs over there," pointing to a block of apartments. "In the Johnston, Mooney and O'Brien shop. Of course, it's long gone now."

"Pity it's gone," said Gary. "I'm starving. An éclair now would be just heaven."

"Did you not have your lunch?" asked Julie, with concern.

"Oh yes, but once someone mentions food my juices get going, you know what I mean?"

Vinny laughed loudly. "My ma calls me a dustbin, I eat so much."

They passed over the main road at Ballsbridge and continued down along by the river.

"Is it much further?" asked Peter.

"No, just on down to Ringsend, why?" said Vinny, a little annoyed.

"It's just that I was playing football yesterday and I hurt my big toe off a wall."

"You're supposed to kick the ball, not the wall," said Vinny with a snigger.

Peter didn't complain any more after that.

"The tide is very far out," Julie remarked as they passed along the small granite-topped wall at Sandymount Strand.

They could see oyster-catchers probing the sand for food. Black-headed gulls screamed overhead. A light breeze blew off the sea.

"There's his house." Vinny pointed across the road. "The one with the red door."

They ran across the road. A car screeched and the driver honked his horn. "You shouldn't be driving so fast," Vinny shouted after him.

Arriving at the hall door, Vinny gripped the brass knocker then rapped once. They waited several moments but there was no answer.

"Knock again," said Gary.

"Maybe he's asleep," suggested Julie.

Vinny flicked up the letterbox. They could hear loud music.

"That's opera," said Peter.

"We all know that, know-all!" Vinny hammered twice with the knocker. "I think he's coming." They stood in anticipation. The door opened a little.

"Push," said a voice from behind the hall-door. They all pushed hard, then the door swung wide open and they collapsed on the floor. The man laughed warmly.

Uncle Tommy was a tall man with steel-grey hair. Heavy-set eyebrows behind thick horn-rimmed glasses gave him the appearance of a great horned owl. He wore a fawn woollen cardigan, grey slacks and a pair of highly-polished black shoes.

"Good afternoon," said Uncle Tommy. "Sorry about that door, it gets very stiff from the damp."

"Hello, Uncle Tommy. These are my friends Julie Brady, Peter Weir and Gary Watson," said Vinny.

"Not the Watsons from Pembroke Cottages?"

"Yes, my grandmother lives there; we live in Belmont Crescent."

"Come in, come in," said Uncle Tommy warmly. He pulled out his handkerchief and blew his nose, went inside into the sitting-room and stopped the record-player. He blew his nose again. "That was the great Joseph Schmidt, who was known as the pocket Caruso. The poor man had a tragic life. He was only thirty-eight when he died, back in 1942."

"Oh, that's nice," said Peter. "I mean the music, not that he died."

"Do you like opera, young man?" asked Uncle Tommy.

"Well, my da plays it sometimes instead of the Beatles or Elvis."

"My ma sent you this." Vinny presented the rhubarb tart to his uncle. There was several cracks in the pastry. "Oh, sorry about that," said Vinny. "It was perfect when I left the house."

"Your mother is a walking angel. Now, I'll just slip it into the oven for a few minutes then we can all have some with tea, later. Does that suit everyone?"

"Oh yes," they all replied. They watched Uncle Tommy go to the kitchen carrying the tart. They looked at each other and grinned.

After a few moments he returned. "Sit down, sit down, don't stand on ceremony around here. Just put those papers and magazines on the floor beside you, Jane."

"Julie," she corrected him.

"Oh, Julie, sorry about that. Well, Vinny tells me you want to start a horror club." They all nodded in agreement. "Well, the first thing you'll need is premises."

"Yes," said Vinny. "We thought about our bedrooms, but sometimes our interests may conflict with the rest of the family, namely one twenty-one-year old sister called Amanda, if you know what I mean."

"Indeed I do," said Uncle Tommy. "So I've been thinking long and hard since your phone call, and I've decided that I have just the thing for you." He smiled at their surprised faces. "Just follow me."

They watched him go into the kitchen and open the back door to the garden.

"Go on," said Vinny to the others.

Uncle Tommy stood in the middle of his well-cared-for garden and pointed to an old railway carriage. "What do you think of that?" he asked, patting his chest with his two hands.

"You mean we can use it for our club?" asked Vinny.

"Of course," said his uncle. "If it suits," he added, smiling.

They entered the carriage.

"It's deadly," remarked Peter.

"Oh, it's quite safe, I assure you. I used to use it as a workshop when I made the occasional bookcase or stool."

"No, he means it's great," said Julie.

"Oh, I see, very good . . . not quite up to the latest slang."

"What's slang?" asked Peter.

"Get a grip," said Gary.

"Just what you said," said Julie.

They looked around. It was perfect for what they wanted. The seats had been removed. There was a table, some chairs, a filing cabinet, shelves filled with craftsman's tools and old bottles, tins of varnish and glue, and the smell of beeswax and turpentine.

"Thanks a million, Uncle Tommy."

"Yes, thanks, Mr Quinn."

"Think nothing of it, I'm glad it will be used. Your dad and I had lots of fun here when we were kids. But there are two rules: no smoking, and turn off the lights when you're finished."

"Oh, we don't smoke," said Gary, looking very guilty.

"Let's check on that tart, it should be warm by now." They sat around having tea and tart with a dollop of ripple ice cream on it. "I have a weakness for ice cream," said

Uncle Tommy. "I got it from my mother. She always bought it for us on Sunday as a special treat, when we were small."

Peter spied a stack of film posters and stills on the floor beside Uncle Tommy's armchair. "That's a deadly poster you gave Vinny from the film *The Skull*," he said.

"Oh yes, we showed that in the 'shack" where I was a projectionist, you know."

"The one with Peter Cushing and Christopher Reeve," added Gary.

"It's Christopher *Lee*! They're just learning," said Vinny.

"The shack?" asked Julie.

"Well, you probably know it as the Ritz," he added. They all looked blank. "The Oscar, then?"

"Oh yes, I think I heard of that," added Gary.

"No, of course you would all be far too young to remember the Ritz, or the Sandford for that matter. That was another cinema I worked in. Most of my collection of posters and film stills came my way because they closed the picture houses down and a lot of that material was being dumped."

"Dumped?" said Julie. "That's terrible."

"Nobody wanted them except me," he smiled.

"Some of these old posters had very good artwork especially the American ones," Uncle Tommy added.

"Nowadays people collect things like call cards," said Julie.

"Well, I went through my collection and came up with a few interesting posters and stills for you. But be careful with them, they are old and they tear easily."

"We will," said Vinny. "Thanks a million."

"Your mother doesn't mind you starting this club?"

"Oh no, she knows it's only harmless fun, but she thinks that kind of film and book is revolting."

Uncle Tommy smiled broadly. "My favourite posters are from the westerns and the epics. They don't make pictures like that any more," he sighed. "The great thing about videos is you can build up a good collection of old pictures." Uncle Tommy poured himself another cup of tea, then waved the teapot. "More?" he asked.

"No, thanks," said Julie, speaking for the others.

"You need the tea when you're chatting, it keeps you lubricated," he chuckled.

"Tell them about some films, especially the Dracula ones," Vinny suggested.

Uncle Tommy sat back in his chair and lit his pipe. A plume of grey smoke covered his face. He sucked several times on the pipe, looked at the ceiling in deep thought, then said, as if he was revealing a deep secret: "You know, of course, that *Dracula* was written by an Irishman?" They did, but remained silent, not wishing to interrupt his flow. "Bram Stoker was his name, from Clontarf. That very book, apart from scaring the living daylights out of millions of people, has inspired over seven hundred films, books, plays, comics and paintings. The *Dracula* book itself has been translated into twenty-two different languages."

Julie suddenly produced a notebook and pen from her jacket and began to take notes. "You don't mind?" she enquired.

"No, of course not," said Uncle Tommy, who was enjoying the company and the interest of the young people.

Vinny nodded to Julie in approval.

"Now, the first Dracula film was a silent one; it was made in Germany in 1922. Only it wasn't called *Dracula* it was called *Nosferatu*." Julie made an attempt to spell it. Uncle Tommy moved his head forward towards his attentive audience. "That means 'the undead'." He lit his pipe again. "The main character was called Count Orlok. I'm trying to remember the actor's name . . . now, what was it . . . Max something. Max Schreck, that's it. Then Hollywood made the famous *Dracula* film in 1931 with Bela Lugosi. '*Velcome to Transylvania*'," he said, mimicking the Hungarian actor. "Did you know, before Bela Lugosi died he asked to be buried in his Dracula costume?"

"Maybe he thought he was going to rise again," said Vinny, laughing.

Uncle Tommy's laughter turned into a cough and he coughed uncontrollably for several seconds until Peter brought him a glass of water. "Oh dear, that was a good one all right," he continued to chuckle. "Ah, you can't beat a good laugh, it does you a power of good. Now, where was I? Oh yes, and the other great horror actors were Lon Chaney Jr, John Carradine, Boris Karloff . . . now he was my favourite; he played Frankenstein's monster." Uncle Tommy relit his pipe. "The scariest Dracula must be the *Horror of Dracula* with Christopher Lee and my other all-time favourite, Peter Cushing, who played Professor Van Helsing. I don't suppose you have seen any of those?

"No," said Vinny. "I think some of them are on video."

"Video," smiled Uncle Tommy. "What a great invention. I've made my own small collection, but it's mainly John Wayne and James Stewart."

"Were they ever in any horror films?" asked Peter.

"No," said Vinny. "Don't be so dopey, they're cowboys."

"Well, here are some more stills and posters," said Uncle Tommy. "And remember, they are hard to come by." He carefully unfolded a poster which read *Blacula*.

"Ah," said Gary. "Look! They made a mistake; it should be *Dracula*."

"No," said Uncle Tommy. "This was the first black version of Dracula. Now, here's another good one. A Dracula film from 1979. This had the world's greatest actor, Laurence Olivier, as Professor Van Helsing and Frank Langella as Dracula. You know, I've just remembered there was a French film called *Tendre Dracula*."

"Tender Dracula," said Julie.

"That's right," said Uncle Tommy. "That had Peter Cushing as Dracula . . . not a very successful film, I'm afraid." Uncle Tommy laid out several film stills.

"He looks scary," said Julie, pointing at one picture.

"That's *Nosferatu* from 1979 with Klaus Kinski as the vampire."

"Uncle Tommy, you are a mine of information."

"Your father used to say useless and irrelevant information. Ah sure, it kept me out of the pubs," he smiled.

"They're all deadly," said Vinny as he browsed through the collection. "There must be about a hundred here."

"Can we pin them up?" asked Gary.

"I don't see why not," said Uncle Tommy. "Now, let me see, I have some thumb-tacks around here somewhere in the house . . ."

# Chapter Two

A stout shabby figure hurried up Grafton Street. He didn't want to be late for his appointment in Bewley's. Cars and trucks were still parked on the street so he knew it wasn't eleven o'clock yet, for at eleven the street would revert to being pedestrians only. Passing Brown Thomas he stopped and bought the paper, crossed himself as he looked down at Clarendon Street church, then slipped into Bewley's.

The smell of coffee filled his nostrils; he loved it although he always drank tea. He quickly hurried through the main restaurant area, keeping his eyes straight ahead in case anyone stopped him that he owed money to. But he had no real fears as it was far too early for that lot. In the evening it might be a different story. Turning left he headed for the stairs that led up to the museum. It was always nice and quiet there if you wanted a chat or to read the paper.

He was the first to arrive, which was a great relief to him. Removing his coat and scarf, he sat down at a table and called over to the waitress who was dressed in a period costume.

"A pot of tea, Kay, and one of those sticky buns – thanks. And could you give me a pot of hot water as well? That's the job."

Brendan Doyle was one of the city's opportunists. He could ferret a bargain anywhere. His philosophy was "I must win", whether it was bumming a cigarette from a stranger or striking up a conversation with someone in a café and getting them to buy him tea and possibly a cake, or in the evening touching someone for a pint.

He would leave his flat in the city early each morning with twenty pounds in his top pocket, and endeavour to return home having had several cups of tea, breakfast, lunch and possibly dinner, or tea anyway, without having to break it.

This had taken skill; it involved years of practice. It was an art and he was proud of it. He could even convince some of the street buskers to throw him a few pounds on occasion. He fancied himself as a king stroker, that's what one of his mates called him. But he knew he was not in the same league as the big boys who could stroke the business world. Still, in his pond he was a big fish.

Not that he was afraid to do an honest day's work. He didn't work officially, he lived on social welfare, but he often helped his friend Jimmy to move furniture for people. This could be very lucrative but it was hard work. All that lifting didn't help his bad back. Not that the doctors could ever find anything seriously wrong with it, but what did they know?

Yes, he must always be in a win situation, he constantly

reminded himself, even if it just meant picking up a discarded newspaper from a street bin.

"Excuse me, Kay, any chance of putting a couple of tea bags in the water? The tea is so weak it's afraid to come out," he cajoled.

Kay gave him a refill of tea. He licked his index finger and picked up the remaining crumbs from the plate then, popping it in his mouth, he sucked his finger.

He checked his watch. It was twenty minutes past eleven. Still no sign of Doctor Drachler. He hoped he would show, and hoped he would be pleased with his find. He didn't know what kind of doctor this Doctor Drachler was, but he knew it wasn't medicine. He was a cold fish, this Drachler, but he paid well for any item he liked. Doyler knew he had a antique business and that he was some kind of historian, a collector and writer. Someone with a finger in every pie, Doyler surmised.

He hadn't seen him for two years. The last time they did business was when he sold him two gargoyles or demon candlesticks dating back to 14th-century Turkey – or was it Persia – he couldn't remember. They were beautifully carved, he recalled, and made of silver.

They'd been taken from an old canary bird who lived on her own in a big old house in Cork. He had spotted them the day they went to collect the grand piano that she wanted to auction. She died not long after and no one even missed them from the house. He was only sorry he didn't get a few more items. An old woman like that would probably leave her fortune to her cat or dog. People like that didn't know the meaning of poverty; that's how he justified stealing.

It was a stroke of luck he'd happened on this Doctor Drachler. He'd got the tip-off from his mate, Jimmy, who in turn had got the nod from a small antique dealer in the city for whom he collected.

Doyler had been paid five hundred pounds in cash by the old geezer from Romania or Poland or wherever he came from. He would have been happy with two hundred quid. When the doctor saw the silver candlesticks, his eyes lit up. That's when Doyler knew he'd buy them. He just threw out the figure five hundred, assuming that Drachler would beat him down in price; but no, he said nothing, asked him to wait in the pub where they were having their lunch and returned within half an hour with the money.

Afterwards, Doyler was sorry he hadn't asked for more but he thought the guy might have just walked away. Doyler told his friend Jimmy he got two hundred because he knew he would have to give him half of it, and twenty pounds to his dealer for the introduction. Jimmy offered to give twenty-five to Harold, the antique dealer, out of his hundred, so in the end Doyler managed to pocket four hundred quid. Not bad for a day's work.

He smiled, remembering the incident.

"Good morning."

Doyler was so lost in thought he hadn't noticed the doctor arriving. His hand had been fiddling with the yellow carnation on the table and he accidentally snapped the stem and knocked over the vase. The doctor's quick reflexes caught it before it hit the floor.

"Oops, clumsy me," Doyler flashed a broad smile. "Can I get you something?" he asked the doctor.

"Coffee, black." The doctor removed his coat and sat, drumming his fingers on the table.

Doyler hurried back with a mug of coffee. "How was your trip?"

"The plane was delayed in London because of fog."

"It was foggy here last night, but it lifted by morning. Grand day now," remarked Doyler.

"Well, what do you have for me? Your letter was very cryptic."

Doyler found it hard to look directly at the doctor, whose eyes seemed so mesmerising he could almost feel himself locked into their stare. He looked around at the old table, the typewriter, the messenger bike, anywhere but at the doctor.

"I think you will find this very interesting, putting it mildly." He stuffed his hand inside his overcoat and pulled out a plastic bag. The doctor stared at the grotty supermarket bag, wondering how its contents could possibly interest him. Doyler grinned. stuck his grubby hand inside the bag and pulled out a red leather-bound book. The spine was badly damaged and the pages were loose. "This is it!" he beamed proudly.

The doctor looked at it and stared at Doyler. "This is what? You haven't brought me all the way from London to buy a tatty old book?"

"It's not the book but its contents. It's a diary, a journal dating back to 1861."

"You're wasting my time, I have books and manuscripts

dating back to the beginning of the printing press." He sipped his coffee. "Doyle, do you realise you made me miss an important auction taking place in Christies today?"

"Doctor Drachler, the contents of this diary will make you rich with your contacts and all, you being a writer."

The doctor picked up the book and flicked open the pages. The handwriting was very legible. He looked at the date: *November 3rd 1861, Templestown Parish, in the County of Wexford.*

He opened the book at the final entry. It began: "God forgive me but I do not have the courage to do what I must do." Turning back to the beginning of the journal, he read: "Whoever may come upon this journal, please believe that I am of sound mind and that all that I have written down is true, no matter how fantastical or fanciful it may appear. I would not have believed it myself only that I too have seen and witnessed it with my own eyes."

The doctor looked up at Doyler, then opened the journal somewhere in the middle and began to read another snippet. "I have little time to decide upon my course of action. The task I have set myself must be accomplished before sunset . . ." His finger moved down the page, then read "I hope by the power of the written word to make you believe that, as God is my witness, we are cursed by this vile creature, this Nosferatu, this vampire . . ."

The doctor closed the journal and took a deep breath. "Where did you come upon this journal?"

"Sorry, doctor. Like the journalists, I cannot reveal my sources."

The doctor picked up the journal. "This is very interesting indeed."

Doyler was clearly relieved by the remark and ordered more tea and coffee. "Now we'd better get down to brass tacks." There was an air of confidence about him as he lit a cigarette. "I reckon something like this is easily worth at least five hundred pounds." The doctor stared hard at him. Doyler became uneasy again. "Well, I know it's only a book and it's not in very good condition, but it's the content that matters. A man like you could turn this into gold bars."

The waitress brought over the tea and coffee. "I'm spoiling you," she said, with an edge in her voice. "This is self-service, you know."

"Ah, sure, you're an old pet." Doyler placed two pound coins on the tray. He smelt money so he knew he could afford to be generous this morning.

"Doyle," said the doctor, "I am very pleased with this journal. You have done well to get your hands on it." He reached into the inside of his jacket pocket and pulled out his calf-skinned wallet. Doyler's eyes lit up as the doctor counted out five hundred pounds and threw in an extra fifty. "That should cover the price of the journal and your expenses."

"Very kind indeed," said Doyler as he grabbed the money, then, checking over his shoulders, he quickly put the notes away in his trousers pocket. The doctor got up to leave. Doyler helped him on with his coat and scarf. "Beautiful tweed," remarked Doyler. "Donegal?"

"As a matter of fact, it is."

"Ah, see, I have the eye and the touch. I used to work in a men's clothes shop. That was in the early fifties."

The doctor turned to leave then turned around to Doyler. "I may require your services in the near future, so expect a call."

"At your service, Doctor Drachler, at your service." He watched the tall figure of the doctor leave. "Kay, bring me the biggest chocolate éclair in that case. I feel like treating myself."

# Chapter Three

November 10th 1861, off the coast of County Wexford.

The wind was from the south-west blowing a force six. The rain beat down. Captain Kruger could see worse weather was setting in from the west.

*The Dark Star* was a powerful clipper and could handle well in bad weather, yet he felt somehow the ship was jinxed. He'd had that feeling ever since she sailed out from the West Indies with her cargo, mainly of sugar and coffee, and the crates of soil that he was asked to carry to England by some wealthy botanist.

It seemed a crazy idea bringing dirt from one place to another. Still, he'd been well paid for the task. Some of the crew said there was a bad feeling off the boxes. He had laughed it off initially. However, four of his crew disappeared during the voyage. One body was recovered from the sea. When they took it aboard it was drained of blood and several bite marks were found on the neck. They gave it a decent burial and returned it to the sea.

From then on the normally calm captain, who would put a rueful grin on his wind-coarsened face and squint at bad weather muttering gentle words to his ship and to the sea itself, taking it all in his stride, was close to panic. His grim expression and eyes showed fear as if he knew something the crew could only guess at.

The ship had even been rammed by a sperm-whale. This was very frightening for the crew members. Luckily, no damage was done. The captain put it down to the fact that it must have been a female who thought they were a whaling ship, and she was protecting her young. Even the dolphins who normally would follow the ship and swim alongside her did so only briefly before hurrying away. Captain Kruger wondered could wild creatures sense things that humans were slow to notice?

Soon the wind was blowing up to force eight, the waves responding and reaching heights of fifteen feet. The winds seemed to be increasing all the time. Now they were driving into the teeth of the storm. The waves rose up to thirty feet. It seemed as if water and wind were conspiring to wreck their vessel. Visibility was very poor yet he could see the gleam of the lighthouse, a welcome beacon in this deadly storm.

"Eddystone lighthouse!" he bellowed, and turned into what he believed to be Plymouth Sound. Moving into the open mouth of the bay, they could feel the power of the heavy sea setting in towards the shore. The continual indraught and the strong winds turned this into a mariner's nightmare as they tried to steer a course.

"Captain, Captain, this is not Plymouth Sound," yelled a crew member. "It's Hook tower. We're in Ireland!"

"Damn!" shouted the captain as he attempted to turn the clipper and free her from the storm's grasp.

There was a terrible scream followed by the sound of someone going overboard. The captain turned to find a tall man standing alongside him wearing a black cloak. His eyes glowed a hellfire red.

"What the devil . . ." Suddenly the captain felt an iron grip on his throat. The stranger flashed a deadly grin, revealing two long wolfish fangs. The crew heard a unearthly scream. They knew it was the captain.

From a small cottage, a man watched in horror as the ship turned broadside then impaled herself on the rocks.

Early next morning the sea was calm. The man from the cottage hurried down to the shore. In among the indented inlets and rocks he saw the broken masts and hulk, floating timber and rigging, cargo boxes and dead bodies washed to the shore. This was not the first time Mad Tom had seen a wreck in these waters. It was known locally as the graveyard of a thousand ships – frigates, merchant vessels and other sailing ships had been lured to their end along this coast. The last one was only a few weeks earlier, at Lucifer Shoals, off Rosslare Point.

Still, one man's tragedy could be another one's gain. He rummaged around and searched the dead bodies for valuable items. Some wore rings, others had attractive daggers and muskets. The belts and buckles could easily be resold. Mad Tom kept checking over his shoulder, for if any other villagers saw the disaster they would be down here like vultures picking over the remains. No one liked to hear of such a tragedy, but that was fate, and if he didn't help himself, others quickly would.

It was still very early, the sun was not long up. His biggest fear was the peelers and Father Funge. If Father Funge saw him robbing the dead he would put his priest's curse on him. Mad Tom filled his sack then checked some of the boxes. They were marked "coffee".

There were six long coffin-like crates lying beside each other in a small cave. Mad Tom wondered how they had all washed up such a neat way on the dry sand. They must have been pulled up, he thought to himself, but how? He was the first to reach the shore. He tried to open them with his bare hands but could not budge the lids. He would try later, bring down the horse and cart and take what he could manage. There were other bodies to search that would have purses and sovereigns, he hoped.

Turning over one of the bodies, he stepped back in shock, for the face had a most terrifying expression and the eyes were still open. Mad Tom noticed the throat of the man was torn open. It was as if those dead eyes and the twisted expression on the face were attempting to yield up some terrifying secret the sailor had seen before his horrifying end.

Mad Tom had heard in the shebeen that the eyes of a murdered man kept the image of his murderer in them. He stooped down to have a closer look but could see only the blank stare of a dead man.

The other body in the rock pool had similar lacerations to the neck.

Mad Tom became very nervous as he rummaged through the pockets. He found a watch and a compass. As he began to search the inside pocket, a large crab sidled out from the waistcoat. Mad Tom recoiled in terror and fell back on the rough rocks. The barnacles grazed his palms. Gulls screamed overhead and heavy dark clouds gathered from the sea. Mad Tom spat on his palms and began to stagger with his booty over the rocks.

A loud clap of thunder startled him, making him lose his footing. He fell face-down on to another dead body. There was seaweed across the face. The mouth gaped open as if in silent scream. A smaller crab crawled out of the open jaws. This sent Mad Tom into an even greater panic. He gave out a loud yell, grabbed his sack and ran as fast as he could up to the roadside. His heart pounded and his breathing was heavy.

Bending over, he began to take deep breaths to recover himself. Still no one was about. He swung the sack over his shoulder and headed for his cottage. His nervousness turned into giddiness and he began to laugh uncontrollably. He laughed so hard, tears streamed from his eyes. When he got to the cottage he quickly entered and shooed two cats off the table. He lifted the milk jug and the bread and put them on the sideboard then spilled the contents of the bag on to the table.

This was his lucky day indeed. He began to carefully finger a gold watch, a dagger, three rings, the leather belts, a small compass, a necktie and two purses full of coins. The watch pleased him the most. He pressed it open. Water dripped from inside it. There was an inscription on it which he couldn't read. He shook it several times in an effort to rid it of the water, then placed it on the mantelpiece. He began to count the coins.

Outside the rain began to beat hard against the window.

Mad Tom had just finished some boiled pigs' feet. He gulped down a mug of tea, draining it to the end. He picked the tea leaves from his tongue. The cats sprang on to the table and began to lick and chew on the pig bones, taking the delicate morsels of fat and meat that he had missed. He began to stroke them with his greasy fingers and hoist them a little from the table with a grip on their tails. "Maybe I could teach you two how to dance and I could earn a few shillings out of you."

Wiping his hands, he took up the fiddle he kept on the dresser and began to play a reel. Louder and louder he played until the little cottage echoed with the music. Once he'd take up the fiddle he'd play a frantic style, as if possessed by a demon. The locals had nicknamed him "Mad Tom" because of this. They could hear him day or night from the roads, the fields or the meadows. He'd even silence the corncrakes in summer, remarked one villager to another when he was in earshot.

Mad Tom didn't care; nothing bothered him, he kept himself to himself. Up from the chair he leapt and danced around the table, kicking his legs in the air and playing as loud as he possibly could, swinging about until he collapsed back on a soft armchair he had found at another wreck near Rosslare.

The cats sprang off the table and stood at the front door. "What is it, my sweeties, expecting company? Or do you want to earn your keep and go a-ratting?" Suddenly they bolted under the armchair. "What is it? Is it that bloody dog belonging to the Whelans, that mangy cur? I swear I'll kill that dog if it comes around here again." Mad Tom grabbed up his stick, pulled open the front door, staggered out and circled the cottage. There was no sign of the dog. "Just as well," he growled at the gathering darkness. "If it comes near this place," he swore again, "I'll crush its skull and leave the carcase to be picked clean by the ravens."

Mad Tom had good reason to be bitter about that dog. He had lost four sheep to it. He'd bought them at a fair in Gorey one Saturday. By Sunday they lay dead, torn asunder by the dog. Mad Tom had confronted Whelan about his savage mutt. Whelan was a gamekeeper and the landlord he worked for liked the dog because it was the finest otter hunter in these parts, so Mad Tom got no satisfaction from either of them. Admittedly, he was given a present of four goats by Whelan which turned out to be more useful to Mad Tom in the end.

He tapped the nearby gorse bush just in case it was hiding, but there was no sign of the dog. Perhaps a fox or a badger had come sniffing by the cottage. That must have been why the cats had gone crazy, Mad Tom reasoned with himself.

When he reentered the cottage, he nearly passed out with fright. Standing in the kitchen was a tall thin man with a pale face and long black curly hair. He wore a black cape over a black suit. Mad Tom stood trembling in the doorway. The fire threw a warm glow across the stranger whose eyes seemed to flame red when he saw Mad Tom.

"Pardon my intrusion," said the stranger. His voice was well-modulated with a hint of a mid-European accent.

Mad Tom relaxed his grip on his stick. "We don't normally get such a fine sort of gentleman around these parts. Are you lost, sir?" he enquired.

"I was heading for England but our ship was wrecked last evening."

Mad Tom looked over at all the items he had stolen off the drowned crewmen's bodies, hurried past the stranger to the table and, with one movement of his arm, quickly swept all the objects into his sack.

"Sit down," beckoned Mad Tom, "and I'll give you a bite to eat."

"That is very hospitable of you but I am not hungry."

"A nice mug of tea, perhaps?"

"Have you any wine, preferably red?"

"Lord, no, there isn't any of that kind of finery around here. A drop of poitín perhaps, the finest in the area?"

"A glass of water would suffice."

Mad Tom quickly scooped some water out of a bucket

into a tankard. "Finest water in these parts, from a well out the back."

The stranger lifted up the tankard. Engraved on the front was *The Golden Star*.

Mad Tom stared at him. "Ah yes, I found that on the strand near Baginbun Head. There was a shipwreck there, when was it . . . ?" He scratched his stubble. "Yes, December, not long after Christmas, last year. Providence has supplied me with many a stick of furniture and other useful objects." Mad Tom made himself tea then sat across the table from the stranger. He felt a certain unease with him but tried not to show it. The cats could not be seen anywhere.

"I wonder, could you assist me?" said the stranger quietly. His eyes seemed to lock on to Mad Tom's.

"I will try," said Tom. "What is it you want?"

"Let me explain. I was coming from the West Indies on the clipper *The Dark Star*, returning to England with my relations, when we got caught up in a horrific storm and you know the rest."

"You are the only survivor?" asked Tom. "Your relations all drowned?"

"Not exactly," said the stranger. "They were already buried in the West Indies but I had them exhumed. Their last dying wish was to be buried in Europe." Mad Tom remembered seeing those strange boxes on the shore but said nothing. "Do you know any place they could be buried around here? Preferably a cemetery away from the village."

Mad Tom scratched his head then said, "I know just the place, not too far from here, a lonely cemetery near an old Cistercian abbey."

"That sounds just right," said the stranger.

"People live in the abbey," Mad Tom added. "But they wouldn't be bothering you. I can get a horse and cart and talk to the local priest about the service."

"There would be no need for a priest," said the stranger firmly. "They had their burial service already. It will be just myself who will say a few words over their remains."

"Well, I can get the horse and cart within the next few days."

"I need it tomorrow," said the stranger. "You will be paid handsomely but I would request you to keep my business strictly confidential. I will return tomorrow after sunset. Be sure the horse and cart are ready." The stranger stood up to leave, then turned around and threw a purse of coins which Mad Tom caught in his sweaty palms. "You will receive the rest when you complete the task. Until tomorrow evening, goodbye."

"Goodbye, sir," said Mad Tom. "Honoured to make your acquaintance."

Mad Tom opened the purse. There were twenty guineas in it. His eyes widened with delight and he hurried out after the stranger to thank him. But he was nowhere to be seen. Mad Tom pulled off his cap and scratched his head in puzzlement. A queer sort of chap, he thought to himself. Still, he paid well, that was the main thing.

Returning to the house, he knelt down and put some more logs on the fire. The two cats appeared alongside

*"I know just the place, not too far from here,*
*a lonely cemetery near an old Cistercian abbey."*

him, purring. "Afraid of strangers, my beauties? Well, to tell you the truth, when I saw him in the cottage I thought he was the devil himself." He laughed broadly.

Mad Tom sat shivering in the cart, holding the reins tightly. The horse seemed very nervous and kept moving its head from side to side then up and down. It began to stamp the ground with its front leg.

"What's the matter, Capall? You'd prefer to be in your warm stable than out on this chilly evening? I don't blame you one bit. I wish I was down in the shebeen swilling a pint or two."

The moon hung low in the sky, black clouds scurried by. Mad Tom began to rub his arms up and down, wondering what was keeping the foreigner. He thought he heard a swish of wings, like a big bird. Maybe one of those grannyfishers, he grumbled to himself – that was the local name for the grey heron. Still, he couldn't see any bird. Suddenly the horse began to rear.

"Steady on, Capall, what's wrong with you at all?"

Without warning the stranger was there, standing before him, holding the bridle and calming the horse. Mad Tom had not noticed the stranger approach and, when he saw him, he nearly collapsed with fright. "I declare to God, stranger," he stammered. "You have a way of sneaking up on people . . . like a stoat would sneak up on a hare."

"Let's go," said the stranger, taking long strides down the dirt-track.

Mad Tom leaped off the cart, tied the reins to a fence and hurried after the man. "Pardon my saying," said Mad Tom, as he tried to keep up with the stranger, "but would it not have been easier to collect those coffins or caskets during the day? I mean, you could break your ankle climbing around these sharp rocks at this hour."

The stranger walked silently ahead. The wind picked up. Mad Tom fell behind. He watched the stranger's black cloak blow up in the air, giving the impression of large black wings. The stranger stopped a few hundred yards down and pointed at the large crates. "As you can see, there will be no need to climb down over the rocks. I brought them up." Mad Tom could not believe his eyes. Those crates would take two, maybe four, strong men to haul them up from the shore. "Bring the horse here," commanded the stranger.

"Yes, squire, right away."

Mad Tom hurried away into the darkness. He quickly returned with the horse and cart, hoping that poor old Capall would be able to pull those heavy crates to Tintern Abbey. Mad Tom went to lift one side of the crate; he could barely budge it. "What's in it, rocks?"

The stranger stared hard at him, then lifted the other end of the crate as if it was a box of oranges. Together they hoisted the crates on to the cart. When they had finished, Mad Tom threw an old rope from one side of the cart to the other. "We don't want them falling off, now do we?" said Mad Tom, trying to make conversation.

"Let's go," ordered the stranger brusquely.

Mad Tom lashed the horse with his hazel rod. The horse whinnied, then went cantering down the dirt road. Mad Tom kept glancing at the stranger but his cold eyes just stared forward.

As they passed a small wood Mad Tom saw a movement

up ahead. At first he thought it was a fox or a blue hare, then he realised it was a dog, the same dog that had killed his sheep. He pulled the horse to a sudden halt. The horse reared.

"What the devil are you doing?" asked the stranger. There was great anger in his voice.

"It's that bloody cur of a dog. The same dog that killed my sheep, probably heading to my cottage to kill my hens or goats. I can't have that happening." Mad Tom's voice trembled with anxiety.

The stranger took a deep breath then commanded him not to move. In one movement, he leaped off the cart and plunged into the woods after the dog. Mad Tom roared after the stranger, "He snuck in beyond the Scots pine." Mad Tom sat anxiously in uncomfortable silence, wondering what was going on. Surely the stranger didn't think he could outrun and catch a dog in those dark woods. He scratched hard at his cheek. "It must just be a call of nature. These gentlemen are very polite about things like that."

There was a shuddering cry, like a rabbit caught in a snare – only worse. Mad Tom bit his tongue in fright. "Ouch, that hurt!" He put two dirty fingers in his mouth and gently rubbed his tongue.

He felt a chill of apprehension as he saw the stranger returning from the woods. He was carrying the dead dog. The stranger threw the corpse on the side of the road. Mad Tom stared in terror at the stranger whose eyes blazed back. "You will have no more trouble from this mangy dog." Mad Tom looked down at the dog. Its throat was torn open, just like the crew of *The Dark Star*.

Mad Tom swallowed hard. "I think we'd best be going." The stranger hopped up beside him. From the corner of his eye, Mad

Tom noticed beads of blood trickle down the side of the stranger's lips. "Did you cut yourself?" he enquired nervously.

"I'm all right," replied the stranger. "Let's complete our task before dawn." He pulled out a white handkerchief and dabbed his lips.

They arrived at the cemetery beside Tintern Abbey. Mad Tom tied up the horse, took his spade and began to dig. The ground was hard and he kicked the spade deeper. The stranger took the spade from him and began to dig. Within an hour he had several holes dug. Using ropes, the two men lowered the crates into the individual graves. The stranger handed the spade back to Mad Tom, who began to cover the crates with soil.

The first rays of light appeared in the eastern sky when Mad Tom spat on his hands. "That's it! All done." He grinned a toothless grin. The stranger threw him another purseful of guineas.

"Thank you kindly, stranger, it's been a pleasure doing business with you. Oh, I never got your name?"

"Count Vedil," said the stranger coldly.

"I'm Thomas Roche, people around here call me Mad Tom. Because I like to keep to myself."

"I think you should leave, now," commanded Count Vedil. "I will be staying around these parts for some time. I may call again if I need your assistance."

"Can I give you a lift to the village?"

"No!" A cock crowed in a nearby farm. "Now, leave!" the count snapped.

Mad Tom stuffed the purse into his trousers pocket and hurried to his horse and cart. "Come on, Capall. Let's get out of here."

*They arrived at the cemetery beside Tintern Abbey.*

# Chapter Four

Doyler sat in the snug of Mulligan's pub with his mate Cooley Collins. "A Paddy for me, and a pint of stout for my dear friend, Mr Collins."

"You're in great form tonight, Doyler. Did you win the Lotto or something?"

"I wish," smiled Doyler, as he placed a ten-pound note on the ledge. "Well, to let you in on a secret, I came in for a little windfall, if you receive my meaning."

"What? Did someone die and leave you something?"

"No, no," grunted Doyler. " Let's just say I made a small killing . . ."

"Oh God, I hope you aren't that desperate for a few bob."

"It's a figure of speech, you gombeen."

"I know it is," snapped Cooley. "I was just making a joke."

The drink arrived and Doyler knocked it back in one gulp. "You'd better bring me a pint of stout as well."

"Are you going to keep me in suspense all night, or are you going to tell me about your windfall?"

Doyler lit up a cigarette and took a deep drag. "Ah,

that's grand," he smiled broadly. The grey smoke billowed from his nose and mouth.

"It's like mining for gold, trying to get information out of you."

Doyler grabbed Cooley by the lapel of his jacket and pulled him closer. "Tell me, Cooley, do you believe in vampires?"

"What sort of a question is that? Have you lost your marbles or what?" Cooley pulled away and sipped his pint. Doyler laughed loudly and began to cough.

"Here, give up those fags or you'll kill yourself," snapped Cooley.

Doyler recovered himself with a swig of his pint. With the froth still on his lips, he prodded Cooley with his fingers. "It's not me who's lost his marbles but this foreign geezer who paid me a cool five hundred pounds for an ancient journal written over a hundred years ago in Wexford."

Cooley's eyes widened. "And?"

"It was some story about a vampire that stalked the place, killing villagers and townsfolk."

"Sounds to me like they were dipping into the poitín a little too much," said Cooley.

"A load of superstitious humbug," added Doyler. "But so what? This eccentric foreigner, who's a bit of a historian and antique collector and writer all rolled up in one, was happy to part with all that money for it. Admittedly, I gave him a good selling pitch. I would have taken anything for it. Fifty quid, even. You wouldn't get a fiver for it in a second-hand bookshop."

"There's no doubt about it, Doyler, you are some operator."

"Years of practice," he grinned slyly.

Amanda Quinn entered the pub with her friend Helen. The place was very busy. She looked around for her boyfriend, Tony, the barman. Suddenly Amanda was grabbed by the waist from behind. She gave a shriek.

"How is my little daisy?" grinned Tony. "Not that little," he added.

"Watch it," she retorted in friendly tones.

"How's Helen?"

"Grand, Tony," giggled Helen.

"Busy enough tonight," Amanda remarked. "For a Tuesday."

"Amanda and I just came in for one drink. We were thinking of going to the pictures."

"What are you going to see?" Tony enquired.

"I dunno," said Helen.

"You're gas," said Tony. "If I was going to the movies I'd know what was on, who was starring in it, and have some idea what it was like. Unless, of course, I was with Amanda in the back seat, then I wouldn't care what was on." He squeezed Amanda. "Isn't that right, hotlips?"

"You're supposed to be working, not chatting up the customers."

"Yer right, I'd better go. Meet you for lunch tomorrow."

"Tony, get's two glasses of lager. We'll be over in the snug. See you tomorrow. He's some tulip . . . forgets to get his girlfriend a drink."

"Ah, he's very nice," said Helen. "You're lucky to have

a bloke with a sense of humour. Remember Brian, that I went out with for eight months? That guy hadn't a funny bone in his body. Oh, he was good-looking and had a good job as an accountant. But he was a total drill at times. He'd do your head in . . . I got fed up with his sulking. Let's not talk about him, I'll only get annoyed."

As they pushed open the door of the snug Doyler's eyes widened. "Here come the girls!"

Helen and Amanda threw a polite glance at them and sat down at the table.

"If I were only twenty years younger," Doyler elbowed Cooley. "Would you young girls allow an old man with snow on the roof but fire in the hearth to buy you a drink?"

"No, thanks," said Amanda. "We've ordered."

Tony arrived back with their drinks. "There you are, girls; compliments of the house, well, compliments of me. And there's some nuts to chew on."

"Thanks, Tony." Amanda gave him a loving smile.

Doyler picked up on the expression. "Would that Tony fellow be your boyfriend?"

"Yes, as a matter of fact he is," said Amanda curtly.

"Young love, isn't it grand . . . in our day, we were afraid to look at a girl in case we'd go to hell." Doyler laughed broadly.

The girls ignored them and began to talk together.

Cooley took off his baseball cap and scratched his head. "I still can't believe it. That some bloke would pay that kind of money for a vampire story."

Doyler emptied his glass.

"Excuse me," said Amanda. "I couldn't help overhearing. Are you interested in that kind of thing, mister?"

"I never speak to strange women," grinned Doyler.

"The name's Amanda and this is my friend Helen."

"What kind of things?" Doyler looked at her.

Amanda gave a broad embarrassed smile. "It's just my little brother . . . he's obsessed with all those creepy things, like vampires. In fact, he never shuts up about them. I think it's a bit unhealthy, myself."

"Ah sure, he could be down a lane smoking or worse," Helen remarked. "It's only silly nonsense."

"Sure, I know," said Amanda. "But if I were to tell him I met someone who wrote a vampire story and got paid for it, he would be very impressed."

"Hold your horses, my dear," said Doyler, laughing. "I'm no writer, the only time I hold a pen is to do a crossword or place a bet." Doyler was pleased to get the attention of two pretty young girls. "Before I tell you this remarkable tale," he grinned, "you will allow me to wet my whistle and buy you charming ladies a glass of ale?" He stuck his head around the glass partition and yelled at the young barman.

Tony arrived and took the order. He looked a little annoyed at Amanda, who was sitting close to the older man.

When he returned with the order, he said in an aside to her: "I thought you two were going to the pictures?"

"We've changed our minds," said Helen, smiling.

"Now, as I was saying . . ." Doyler began telling them about the journal. The girls sat silently, hanging on to his every word. When he had finished the girls took a deep breath.

"That's the scariest thing I ever heard," said Helen. "What happened to Mad Tom?"

"It's all a load of old cobblers," said Cooley.

"You tell it very well, Mr . . . eh?"

"Doyle. People call me Doyler. I'm not saying I believe all this," Doyler said in confidence, "but 'there are more things in heaven and earth . . .' as the great Shakespeare once wrote."

"'Than ake dreamt of in your philosophy'," Cooley added. Doyler looked a little annoyed at Cooley for finishing the quotation. "You're not the only one with a bit of culture," Cooley laughed.

The girls laughed warmly. Suddenly the snug door opened and Doyler looked up. The blood seemed to drain from his face.

"What's the matter with you?" said Cooley. "You look like you've seen a ghost. We're full in here, mister," said Cooley to the stranger.

Doctor Drachler ignored the remark and moved towards Doyler.

"Doctor Drachler," he stammered. "What a pleasant surprise. Eh, how did you find me?"

"That does not matter," he said coldly. "I need your services next weekend. I am returning to London tonight. Will you be available?"

"Yes," said Doyler. "Always at your service." Then he added nervously, "If the price is right."

"I need you to travel to Wexford. Bring an assistant."

Doctor Drachler looked at the two young girls. They seemed to become locked in his stare.

Doyler broke the spell. "These are Amanda and Helen, friends of mine."

"Delighted to meet you," said Doctor Drachler, taking Amanda's hand and formally kissing it.

Amanda felt uncomfortable in his presence.

"This is Cooley," added Doyler. "He'll travel with me to Wexford."

"Well, I must be away. I will meet you at the National Gallery at ten o'clock on Saturday, in the restaurant."

"An early start," Doyler smiled. "Oh, don't worry, we'll be there."

Doctor Drachler turned and left.

"Yer man is like something out of one of those old horror movies," Cooley suggested.

"Handsome man," Helen added, "but a little weird."

"That's because we've been listening to all that stuff about vampires," Amanda remarked. "You've gone silent, Mr Doyle."

"Oh, I just wasn't expecting him." He rubbed at his nose nervously. There was a long silence.

"Well, we're off," said Amanda, draining her second glass of ale. "Nice to meet you, Mr Doyle, and your friend."

"You girls wouldn't care for a little supper?"

"No, thanks," said Helen. "Bye!" The girls left the snug.

Amanda walked over to Tony. "Goodnight, see you tomorrow."

"Oh yeh," said Tony. "I hope you had a nice evening."

"You're not jealous of those two old geezers?"

"Of course not," snapped Tony. "Here, give us a kiss."

She kissed him affectionately. "Bye, Tony. See you tomorrow."

As they left the pub, the two girls broke into loud laughter. "Care for a little supper?" said Helen in mocking tones.

"Yes, but not with you, you old git!"

Helen staggered. "These new shoes are killing me," she said.

"Come back to my house and we'll get a Chinese takeaway. I'll ask my da to drive you home."

A light rain began to fall as they headed home. Amanda put her arm around Helen and the two of them began to sing "I'm singing in the rain . . ."

Mrs Quinn looked up from the couch. She put away her knitting. "You girls are back early. I thought you were going to the pictures."

"No, we changed our minds and went for a drink in Mulligan's."

"I wonder why," said Mrs Quinn. "I don't suppose it was because a certain Tony Farrell was working there?"

"I'm starving," said Amanda, ignoring her mother's remark.

"I'll go out and make supper . . ."

"No, Ma, we're going to order a Chinese takeaway. Would you like something?"

"No, thanks, not at this hour."

Vinny came rushing down the stairs. "Ma, have you seen that book *The Undead*? The one I got today?"

"It's where you left it, in the kitchen. You shouldn't be wasting your money on that nonsense."

"You don't understand, Ma . . ."

"Vinny, darling brother, would you be a pet and go around to the Chinese takeaway and get us two spring rolls and curried chips?"

"It's a bit late for him to be going out . . . why don't you phone your order?"

"Ma, I'm thirteen and it's nearly the summer holidays."

"He's big enough," said Amanda. "Here, there's the money. Get yourself whatever you want." Then she added, "If you're quick, I'll tell you something very interesting."

"Something to do with vampires," added Helen.

"Really?" said Vinny.

"Here's the money. Go," said Amanda.

"Well, I'm off to bed," said Mrs Quinn. "Your father will be late home so don't lock the door. And you come straight back, Vinny."

As Vinny hurried towards The Lotus Flower he wondered what Amanda could possibly know about vampires that he didn't know already. Maybe it was something about a new film or a book. Whatever it was, he couldn't wait to find out.

# Chapter Five

"Why does he want us to meet at the National Gallery?" Gary wondered.

"Maybe he wants to show us some picture," offered Peter.

"Get a grip," said Gary.

"It must be very important if he wants us to meet here," said Julie.

"It's four minutes to ten," said Peter, showing off his new watch.

"When did you get that?" asked Gary.

"Yesterday, from my Uncle Dermod – he's home from Boston for a few weeks."

"It's a lovely watch," said Julie.

"Deadly," said Gary. "Your uncle must be really rich."

"Not really," said Peter. Then he smiled broadly. "Guess what he works at?"

"Is it something unusual?"

"Yes," said Peter.

"Is he in the Air Force in America?"

"No!"

"Is he an actor?" asked Julie.

"No!"

"He's a policeman," said Gary.

"No! Give up?" smiled Peter.

"He works for the FBI?" offered Gary.

"No!"

"He's a musician," said Julie.

"No!"

"Tell us," said Gary, a little annoyed.

"He makes comics."

"Comics!" said Gary in disbelief.

"Yes, comics, not the kids' ones. Ones for teenagers. He draws them."

"You mean he illustrates them," said Julie.

"Same thing," said Peter.

"He must be good," said Gary. "All those artists are deadly." Then he added. "How come you never told us before?"

"I didn't know, my ma never mentioned it. Look, here's Vinny."

"Hi, guys! The Gallery has just opened so we'll sit over there on the seat until we see those two blokes arriving."

"What two blokes?" asked Gary.

"I'll recognise them when I see them," said Vinny with confidence. "One is a big fat guy; his name is Doyler. The other is a small skinny bloke."

"Who are we looking for, Laurel and Hardy?" said Gary.

They all broke into laughter at this. Then Vinny said, "This is all very serious. You won't believe what I have to tell you."

"When are you going to let us in on your big secret?"

"Later," said Vinny. "When things are quiet."

"I brought a Walkman recorder. It has a built-in mike, just in case we have to record anything." Julie smiled, producing the machine.

"That's using the noggin," said Vinny.

"Look," said Peter. "Is that them?"

"They're American tourists," said Vinny. "You can spot them a mile off."

"That's them," said Julie. "Coming through the gate!"

Doyler and Cooley entered the grounds of the National Gallery. "Put a pep in your step," said Doyler. "We don't want to be late."

As they entered, Vinny and the others bunched together with their backs to them. "We'll give them a few minutes, then follow. Now don't look suspicious, just pretend you're regular visitors to the Gallery."

"I was here once on a school tour," said Peter.

"We all were," snapped Gary.

"OK, let's go," said Vinny.

Doyler and Cooley hurried down the corridor.

As they passed the rows and rows of paintings, Cooley called after Doyler. "Those pictures are worth a right few bob. Even the frames are valuable . . ."

"It's true, what my dear mother said, Lord rest her soul," sighed Doyler. "You can't make a silk purse out of a sow's ear."

"What's that remark supposed to mean?" said Cooley, a little annoyed.

"Bedad! All this is new," remarked Doyler as he passed a wide, bright room.

"It's through here," said Cooley. "The restaurant."

Doyler beamed a gap-toothed smile at the Spanish waitress. "Tea for two and two slices of the bakewell tart. Oh, and plenty of cream, have to keep up the cholesterol levels." The waitress gave him a puzzled smile. Doyler scanned the restaurant. "No sign of Doctor Drachler." He gave a deep sigh of relief. "At least we're here first. I don't like being late for that geezer."

Vinny and the others came into the restaurant and quickly threw a glance over towards the two men.

Peter headed straight to the food counter. "Can I have a packet of crisps and a can of Pepsi Max, please?"

"Sorry, we don't sell crisps," said the waitress.

"Do you do sausage rolls?"

"No, I'm sorry," said the waitress.

Vinny joined him. "This is not the local shop. Get a couple of croissants and four glasses of apple juice. Here's the money."

Peter arrived with a full tray back to Vinny, Julie and Gary who were sitting at a table near the two men.

"What happens now?" said Gary.

"We wait, that's part of it."

"When are you going to fill us in on your important information?" asked Julie.

"All in good time," said Vinny.

Cooley nudged Doyler under the table. "Here he is!"

Doctor Drachler arrived and sat down beside them.

"Good morning, dear doctor," grovelled Doyler, then

he elbowed Cooley. "Go and get the doctor a mug of coffee, as black as night."

"I was upstairs looking at the Caravaggio."

Doyler looked blank. "Oh yeah," he said. "What a picture."

Cooley returned with the coffee.

"Do you know Tintern Abbey?" Doctor Drachler asked.

"Well, no," said Doyler. "not being much of a churchgoer."

"The one in Wexford that's being restored?" said Cooley.

"How do you know all this?" Doyler demanded of Cooley.

"Ah, I keep my ear to the ground," Cooley said proudly. Doctor Drachler had a stern expression. "Well," said Cooley, "I go to Wexford at least once a year. A relation took me out to view the restored fortified bridge beside the abbey. It was a Cistercian abbey, built in 1200 AD."

Doyler looked pleased. "See, Doctor, I'm very careful who I work with. Cooley, my partner, has a keen interest in all things historical."

"How long have they been working on the restoration of the abbey?" the doctor asked. There was a sense of urgency in his voice.

"Oh a few years at least," said Cooley. "It's slow, painstaking work. They're all craftsmen on that job, no doubt about it."

"Is it easy to gain access?" asked the doctor.

"No problem at all, you can drive right up to it, if my

memory serves me correctly. Do you mind me asking you a question, doctor?"

Doctor Drachler sipped his coffee, then removed his glasses. "Go right ahead."

Cooley hesitated then glanced at Doyler for approval. "What's the fascination with the vampire story? I mean, anyóne with a degree of sense knows it's all a load of bull." Doyler looked decidedly nervous because of his friend's remark.

"Let me explain," said the doctor calmly. "As you are aware, I am a historian, a writer, a collector of antiques, but I am also an arcanologist. I have a keen interest in past cultures and costumes. Vampirism is part of many ancient cultures; Greek, Romanian, French, to name but a few. So my research helps fuel my writing, so to speak." Then he smiled broadly. "Imagine if one were to come upon an authentic case of a true vampire . . . we could all stand to make a lot of money if the one in County Wexford proved to be genuine."

"That's good, all right," said Doyler. "The bit about us making some big bucks."

"Of course," said the doctor. "We will all share in it." Then his tone changed and he said firmly, "I must have your total commitment and you must promise not to breathe a word of it to anyone. Is that understood?"

"Perfectly, of course." Doyler and Cooley chorused.

"We don't want anyone else finding the remains, now do we?"

"No," said Cooley.

"Definitely not," said Doyler.

"I must leave," said the doctor. "I will meet you at seven o'clock tonight outside the Gresham Hotel. It should not take us more than two hours to get to Wexford."

"That's about right," said Cooley. "Depending on the traffic."

Doyler elbowed him. "The traffic will be fine at that time of evening. I'll bring shovels, torches and something to keep the chill out," he smiled.

Doctor Drachler got up to leave, stopped and looked over at the children. His eyes locked in a stare with Julie. She clicked off her Walkman. The doctor moved towards them. They all began to panic as he reached their table. Julie shoved the tape recorder into her bag in haste, then put the bag on the table. It overbalanced and went crashing down on the tiled floor, spilling out most of the contents.

The doctor stood beside them. "Good morning, children. It's nice to see young people so interested in art that they will give up their Saturday mornings."

"Yes, we love it," said Vinny.

"Can't get enough of it," said Gary.

"My uncle is an artist," said Peter.

"How very interesting." Then, looking at Julie, "Have you a keen interest in art?" His eyes focused on the contents of her bag, strewn all over the floor. She pushed some of the stuff with her left foot under the table then said brightly, "I love Leonardo, Raphael, Donatello and Michelangelo."

"I'm impressed," said the doctor. "So you are a fan of the Renaissance period?"

"Oh, yes," said Peter, "And Beethoven, too."

"Indeed," said the doctor.

Julie reached under the table. Keeping her eyes on the doctor, she began to ram the items back into her bag.

"Allow me to help," the doctor offered.

"No, thanks," said Julie.

He reached down and picked up the tape recorder. "I hope this is not broken."

Julie plucked it from his hand. "No, it's fine, I'm sure. I'm always dropping it, it's very sturdy."

"Well, it has been a pleasure meeting such charming young people. I hope I run into you again." With that, he left the restaurant.

"Thank heavens he's gone," said Gary with a sigh.

"I hope he didn't suspect anything," said Julie.

"Of course not," said Vinny. "Why would he?"

Julie just shrugged her shoulders.

"What did you mention Beethoven for?" Gary asked Peter.

"I dunno, when Julie mentioned the ninja turtles it just came out."

"Beethoven is a dog," snapped Gary. "I saw the movie."

"Are you all a bunch of wallies, or what? Julie mentioned artists, not turtles, and for your information Beethoven is or was a famous composer," Vinny sighed.

"Oh yeah," smiled Peter. "I forgot."

"We'd better go," said Doyler. "I reckon we'll have to stay overnight in County Wexford."

"Surely we'll be able to charge expenses as well," added Cooley.

"Now you're using your loaf," said Doyler. "Besides, if we find these old bones with a stake in them, it will be like hitting the jackpot," he laughed loudly.

"Winning the Lotto," said Cooley. Then Cooley frowned and scratched his head.

"What's the matter?" asked Doyler.

"Well, it may be possible to find some poor unfortunate with a stake through his chest cavity, but that needn't mean he was a vampire."

"What are you talking about?" asked Doyler, getting agitated.

"Hold on a minute and I'll get more tea."

Doyler glanced in the direction of the young people, who immediately turned away. The restaurant door opened and a large group of tourists arrived in. Cooley hurried back with fresh tea.

"Have you noticed those kids over there?" Doyler asked. "They haven't moved since we arrived."

"Ah, don't mind them. I was lucky to get more tea and buns before that busload of French tourists arrived."

"What did you mean about finding a corpse with a stake . . . ?"

"Yes, well, you see, in the nineteenth century, and indeed it probably happened in other centuries . . ."

"Listen, Cooley, I don't want a history lesson, just get to the point. Would you bleedin' tell me what you were about to tell me before you went up for the tea."

"Don't be so edgy," snapped Cooley.

"Sorry, it's that doctor fella, he makes me uptight. I don't know why."

"Anyway, in the old days some people who committed suicide could end up getting a stake driven through their hearts."

Doyler's eyes widened. "Why?"

"Because there was a widely-held belief in those days that, if you killed yourself, you might come back as a ghost, or worse, a vampire."

"How do you know that?" asked Doyler.

"You know me, I read anything and everything."

Doyler grabbed Cooley by the lapels. "Listen! Keep your mouth shut about that. If we find a skeleton with a bit of wood in it, it's a vampire. OK? I don't want to kiss goodbye to a few grand because of you talking about bizarre customs in the nineteenth century."

"OK! OK! You asked me and I told you."

"Let's go," said Doyler gruffly.

"I haven't finished my tea yet."

"Come on," growled Doyler. "We're going to find a vampire, even if I have to dig up a few old bones and stick a stake in them myself." Doyler quickly hurried out the door.

Cooley took a gulp of tea then hurried after him.

"Well, I hope you're all convinced," smiled Vinny. "This is the real thing. Julie, do you think you got it on tape?"

Julie rewound the tape and hit the "play" button. The voices were low, but the doctor's voice could be clearly understood.

"Brill," said Vinny.

"Can you tell us now?" asked Gary. "Or are you going to keep us in suspense for the whole day?"

Vinny explained what Amanda had heard in the pub from the two blokes, Doyler and Cooley, about the mysterious doctor and the journal about the vampire.

"This is really creepy," said Julie. "Do you honestly think there is such a thing as a vampire?"

"There's only one way to find out," said Vinny.

"How?" asked Peter.

"We need to follow them. We have to go to Wexford tonight."

"There's no way my dad will drive us there," sighed Vinny. "Not with the European Cup on."

Julie's father was dead and she knew her mother would not approve of the idea, even though she was always decent about driving them to the cinema or other places.

"How about your da?" he asked Gary.

"No," said Gary. "He'll be in the pub with your da, screaming his lungs out."

"My da is working the weekend shift," said Peter.

"Who else could we ask without them making a federal case out of it?" sighed Vinny.

"We could take a train," said Julie.

"Yes, and how do we get to Tintan Abbey?" asked Gary sarcastically.

"It's Tin*tern* Abbey, and we could hire bikes," Julie retorted.

"That's a good idea," said Vinny.

"I don't fancy riding a bike up to some old graveyard in the middle of the night," said Peter.

"Is the little baby scared?" said Gary, patting him on the head.

"Leave him alone," said Vinny. "I wonder if I could persuade Amanda to ask Tony to bring us."

"What about your Uncle Tommy?"

"No," said Vinny. "He never learned how to drive a car."

"I've got it," said Peter. "I'll ask my Uncle Dermod, you know, who is just back from the States. He's dead on."

"Can we trust him?" asked Gary.

"What do you mean?" said Peter. "He's one of the most honest people you could meet in the whole wide world."

"I didn't mean it that way, dumbo!"

"What he means," said Julie, "is would we be able to tell him the reason we want to travel to Wexford?"

"Of course you could . . . he must be into all this, since he's an illustrator for comics. It might give him some inspiration."

"You never told me you had an uncle who worked on comics," said Vinny.

"Well, I didn't really know until he came home this time and he showed me his artwork. It's deadly!"

"He sounds like he's dead on," said Julie.

"Peter, you ask your uncle," said Vinny. "No, better still, bring him over to the club at lunch-time if he's available and we'll explain it all to him."

Julie looked at the tall, handsome fellow entering the carriage.

"This is Dermod," Peter said proudly.

Dermod smiled warmly. "So you must be Julie." Julie could feel herself blush. They shook hands. "Vinny and Gary?"

"Right."

"This is a grand spot for a club. You're very lucky. I wish I'd had a place like this before I went to the States. It would have made a wonderful studio."

They warmed to Dermod instantly.

"Oh, you can use it any time if you fancy doing a bit of drawing."

"Well, that's very nice, thank you."

"How long are you in the States?" Gary asked casually.

"About twelve years. I left Dublin just after Art College, worked for a while doing odd jobs, then I met this comic writer in Greenwich Village in New York. We got chatting. He asked to see my portfolio. He seemed impressed, and a week later I was illustrating one of his stories. It was a story about a World War One soldier. He was the last one alive in this trench so he crawls into a small tunnel to hide from the Germans. Before he knows it, he's in New York in 1980."

"The tunnel is a kind of time machine, isn't that right, Dermod?"

"Yes, Peter."

"What happens?" asked Julie.

"He tries to convince people how terrible war is but nobody wants to listen."

"That's very sad," said Julie. "I could just imagine it."

"Did you become famous after that?" asked Gary.

"Well, not exactly. The comic won a couple of awards. I haven't been out of work since, touch wood!" He stroked the wooden surround of the window.

"Did you ever draw anything creepy?" asked Vinny.

"Oh, yes. I've worked on vampire stories, werewolf stories, aliens, zombies . . . you name it, I've illustrated it."

"How come you're living in Boston?" asked Gary.

"Well, a lot of Irish live there. But the real reason is that I met this wonderful animator who just happened to be the most beautiful woman on this planet."

"Really?" asked Julie.

"She was to me," Dermod said.

Vinny took a deep breath and said very confidentially, "Suppose we were to tell you that we know of a place where there's a real vampire buried?"

Dermod sat back on the stool and folded his arms. "I'm all ears," he smiled.

"You must promise to tell no one," insisted Gary.

A sudden tap on the carriage door made Vinny jump. Dermod opened the door; it was Uncle Tommy carrying a tray. On it were glasses of orange squash, biscuits and a coffee.

"Here you are," he smiled. "I know all this talking makes people very thirsty. Dermod, I suppose I was right bringing you coffee?"

"Thanks a million," said Dermod lifting the coffee from the tray.

"There's milk and sugar there."

"I like it just the way it is, thanks."

"Well, now, that's something I never got a fondness for, coffee, I mean. I'm a tea man all my life and, you know, I have to have something to nibble as well." Uncle Tommy looked at the others who all stared back silently. "Begob, I get the sense I'm interrupting something very important, so I'll leave. Give me a holler if you want any more." He winked at Dermod and left.

Vinny gulped down the orange squash, then wiped his

mouth. "We overheard an amazing conversation this morning in the National Gallery . . ."

"Shall I play the tape for him?" Julie offered.

"Good idea, put it into the machine and turn it up," said Gary.

"I think she knows how to play a tape," said Vinny.

"Ignore the first bits," said Julie. "It's only us eating and shifting on the chairs."

Dermod listened intently to the three men's voices on the tape. ". . . If the one in Wexford proved to be genuine . . ."

"It's nearly over," said Peter.

"Shush," said Gary. "Let him hear the end of it."

When the tape finished Julie clicked it off. They all stared at Dermod. The smile was gone from his face and his expression had become more serious. He paused for a long time, running his fingers across his lips. "This is quite remarkable indeed. I've never heard anything like it before. Even the whole idea of it could trigger off a very interesting story . . ."

"Would you be willing, I mean, if you were doing nothing tonight . . . ?" Julie hesitated about finishing the sentence.

"To go to Wexford, you mean?"

"Yes," said Peter. "We'd all go. I'd be allowed if you were bringing us. So would we all."

Dermod smiled. "Well, I was going to meet a few people tonight for a chat and a jar." He could easily see the disappointment coming over their faces. "Oh well, why not? But only on condition that you get full permission from your folks."

# Chapter Six

November 15th 1861
Kilmore Quay

The two seafarers staggered out of The Schooner tavern, arms around each other's shoulders. They steered each other down the dark streets, one preventing the other from falling or crashing into the many wooden barrels stacked along the streets. They disturbed a young couple kissing down a dark lane.

"Good night to you, my pretty colleen, good night to you, young man." The older man stopped. "Treat her well," he exclaimed as he pointed a finger at the young man. His words slurred. "I mean it, young fella. I know I'm a bit drunk, but I know what I'm saying. The best time in your life is when you're in love."

The young girl giggled.

"I had a sweetheart once," he said proudly, then added sadly, "but I left her for a fiery and demanding love who can change her mind like the wind, can be as calm as glass and as wild as any savage beast you might encounter in the darkest jungle. We're still wed for over forty years, I may be a bag of old bones but she hasn't aged at all; still as beautiful and dangerous as ever."

"What kind of wife is that," said the young girl coquettishly, "who is such a wild thing and never ages?"

The old man beckoned them from the alleyway. "Come over here and I'll show you."

The young girl broke away from her lover. The old man placed one hand firmly on her shoulder and, with the other, pointed out towards the sea. "That's her," he said proudly. "Bathed in the moon's silvery light."

"You have a right silvery tongue yourself," she retorted.

"Ah, sure, if I was only forty years younger I'd be challenging him for your love."

"Let's go," said the young man, pulling the girl away then hurrying down the street.

"Remember, treat her well, you young buck."

"Goodbye," the girl yelled back.

"Ah, Jacko, you never lost it, the bit of charm."

"Timmy, I meant it. You don't know what you have until you lose it. That's a fact." They continued on their way. "You're a good friend, Timmy," he bellowed at the top of his voice. "You've been with me in the warmest days of summer and the coldest days of winter, now that's a friend."

"Thanks, Jacko."

"I'm hungry. Let's go and get some supper."

"Right you be, let's go down to The Madra Rua. Bridie is sure to have some fish stew on the boil."

"Lead on," said Jacko, linking his friend by the arm.

From the top of the shipyard a tall, dark figure stood

silently watching the young couple strolling down towards the harbour.

"It's all as true as I'm sitting here," said Mad Tom. "He just leaped from the cart like a giant black cat into the woods after the dog. There was a loud scream from the mangy cur and that was it." The crowd looked on in amazement.

"What happened then?" asked another.

"Don't hurry him," said the barman, "in case he forgets any details."

"Thank you, Paddy," said Mad Tom. "Now, the crates almost weighed down the cart. Big long wooden boxes like coffins. Well, they were coffins, really. He told me he wanted to bury his relations back in Europe. The ship was bound for England but he wasn't English, more Polish or something like that. Oh, a true gentleman, but deadly cold eyes, don't you know what I mean."

"Oh we do," said another.

"So I can only assume his family originally came from Eastern Europe and settled in the West Indies. They all must have died mysteriously . . . maybe the plague or cholera, like our own in the past. I don't know how they died, but we buried them up near Tintern Abbey. He paid me handsomely." Mad Tom winked at the barman.

"There's no flies on you, Mad Tom, that's for sure."

Jacko and Timmy entered the tavern. "Salutations," Jacko bellowed. "Two bowls of Bridie's finest fish stew, if you please."

Mad Tom got the whiff of the stew that Bridie carried out on a tray. "Bridie, dear, would you send me out some of that along with some soda bread. I can't resist the smell."

"Keep the chill out," laughed Paddy.

"Too true," said Mad Tom as he dunked the soda bread into his stew.

Jacko and Timmy finished their stew, wiped the inside clean with a piece of crust and let out a satisfied sigh. Bridie moved from behind the counter to collect the empty bowls.

"I didn't enjoy that," said Jacko, holding a poker-faced expression.

"I can see that," said Bridie. "You didn't even leave the pattern on the bowls."

This brought loud laughter from Jacko and Timmy. "Ah, you've met your match there," Timmy quipped. Suddenly the tavern door was flung open. A young, pale man staggered in. All heads turned in his direction. He brushed past some tables, nearly knocking over the tankards with the tails of his jacket.

"Steady on," yelled one of the men sitting near the door.

"What's the matter, son?" the barman enquired. The young man stood trembling, his eyes bulging in their sockets. There was a look of terror on his face.

Bridie came in from the kitchen. "What is it, laddie? Here, have a glass of water."

"He looks like he needs something stronger," remarked Mad Tom.

"Jesus, Mary and holy Saint Joseph," the young man cried. "You can never find the law when you want them."

"Sit down," insisted Bridie. "What's troubling you at all?"

"It was terrible, horrible."

"What was?" asked the barman.

"The two of them lying there dead in the moonlight, eyes staring wide like they had seen something monstrous." He began to sob uncontrollably.

"There, there," said Bridie, putting her arm around him.

The young man raised his head and stared into her eyes. "They had their throats torn out."

Mad Tom nearly fell off the bar stool. Jacko and Timmy stared at each other.

"Do you think it might be the young couple we spoke to earlier?"

"Good God! No!" gasped Jacko.

Mad Tom arrived back at his cottage still trembling from what had happened the previous night. He had stayed overnight in the tavern, terrified to venture out in the dark.

He quickly bolted the cottage door and placed an axe on the table that he had taken in from the outhouse. He was ready to defend himself if the stranger called. He knew that somehow the stranger had been involved with the killings.

Why did he have to open his big mouth and tell everyone in the tavern about what happened after the shipwreck? It wouldn't be long before the peelers or the Army would be sniffing around asking questions.

Mad Tom had bought enough supplies to last him a

month. Maybe it would be all blown over by then. He certainly didn't want the law searching his cottage and finding all the booty he had acquired from the several shipwrecks in the area.

A cat sprang on to his back. Mad Tom gave out a loud yell and knocked over his mug of tea. "Get off, cat!" He yanked the cat from his shoulder and flung it on to the floor. "You nearly gave me a heart attack." The cat looked at him and skulked away under the bed. The other cats, sensing the mood Mad Tom was in, made themselves scarce.

He drummed the table with his fingers, then remembered he had some weapons concealed under his bed. He pulled out the wooden settle-bed, sending the cats scurrying all around the room. Wrapped in sacking was a brown Bess rifle. This he had got from a man from Galway who said it was used by the British soldiers during the American War of Independence. He had a powder horn for the musket, and the leaden balls, but he had no idea how to load it. Still, there was a bayonet attached to the rifle. There was also a Hanger sword, taken from a dead Grenadier by Mad Tom's grandfather, back in 1748. His grandfather had left it to him and he was very proud of it. He gripped the handle of the sword and began to slash out at the air.

Then he made several lunges. "There, you devil, got you! No one messes with Mad Tom." He brought the sword and rifle back to the kitchen table. The cats immediately leaped up on the table and he began to stroke them and scratch them below their ears. "Like that? I'm sorry, my dears, for being so rough with you earlier. Forgive me?" He nosed their fur. "Good. I think this calls for a drink."

Mad Tom opened the cupboard and took out a bottle of brandy, sat back on the chair and started to swig it down. Raising the bottle to the air he toasted the French vessel that had run aground at Baginbun and provided it for him.

Mad Tom slowly lifted his head off the table and wiped the dribbles from his mouth. His left leg had a cramp in it from the way he had been sleeping. He stamped the ground furiously to try to ease it.

"Blast!" The vibration sent the brandy bottle that was lying on its side rolling off and crashing to the floor. As Mad Tom picked up the shattered pieces of glass, he noticed that night had fallen. This made him anxious. Splashing his face with cold water from a basin, he hurried over to the window. The moon hung bright in the sky. He could hear the sound of the sea and he knew the wind was rising. He craned his neck to see if there was anything along the outside wall. Nothing. Then he checked the small window of the kitchen where he could see if anyone was coming up the boreen. All was quiet. He gave a deep sigh of relief.

Then he noticed the cats sitting alert and looking towards the small kitchen window. "What is it, my lovelies?" Mad Tom hurried back to the window, hoping to God it wasn't the peelers. He stared hard down the moon-drenched fields. Then his heart started pounding, for he could see clearly the tall dark form of a man hurrying up the road. In blind panic, he ran around the cottage knocking over stools and stepping on cats' tails. The cats hissed and cowered in corners.

Mad Tom picked up the axe and the sword and hid under the table. He could now hear the sound of footfalls, faint at first but getting louder. Mad Tom had no lamps lit, so the inside of the cottage was quite dark. Perhaps whoever was outside would think there was no one in and leave.

Suddenly the face of a man loomed up at the window. "Holy Mother of God, protect me!" whispered Mad Tom as he sat huddled and trembling under the table. After several moments, he looked up at the window. The face was gone.

Suddenly there was a loud hammering on the door. Mad Tom didn't move. "I know you're in there, Tom. You can't fool me. Now open the door."

Mad Tom recognised the voice. It was Father Funge. Mad Tom quickly hurried to the door and unbolted it. Father Funge, a tall slim figure with wiry grey hair, looked sternly at Mad Tom.

"Thank God it's you," said Mad Tom. "I thought it was . . ." Mad Tom turned away, not finishing what he was about to say.

"Go on, Tom," Father Funge demanded. "Who did you think I was?"

"Eh . . . eh . . . the peelers," he blurted out.

"Don't lie to me." The priest moved into the cottage and sat at the table. "Put on some light," he demanded. Tom quickly lit the oil lamp. The priest looked at the rifle, the sword and the axe. "Expecting trouble?" he asked in mocking tones.

"Ah no, I was just polishing them . . . eh, would you care for some tea?"

The priest shook his head. Mad Tom sat down facing the priest, eyes cast downwards. "I want to know all," insisted the priest. "I hear you were boasting over in Kilmore Quay about some stranger who survived *The Dark Star* shipwreck?"

"How do you know?" Tom asked nervously.

"Never mind how I know," snapped the priest. "But you'd better keep nothing from me, do you hear? Nothing. Look at me," demanded the priest. "Since the Kilmore Quay killings there have been four more in Wexford town, all killed the same way."

"It's nothing to do with me, I don't want to get involved."

"You are involved. I'm not leaving until you come clean. Or, by God, I'll denounce you from the pulpit, and that's a promise."

Mad Tom began to explain how he had first met the strange gentleman and how he'd helped him bury the coffins.

"Where?" asked the priest.

"Near Tintern Abbey."

The priest paused for a few moments. "There's evil abroad these nights and this kind of killing has only happened since the foreigner set foot on our soil."

"Have there been any enquiries from the peelers?" Mad Tom wondered.

"No, there haven't. They've been on the alert since the rumours of a Fenian uprising."

"I can't see that happening," sighed Mad Tom. Then, grinning broadly, he added, "Let's hope it does."

"To more immediate matters. I am calling a meeting at my house tomorrow afternoon at around three o'clock. I want you there."

"But, but . . ." protested Mad Tom. "I don't want to get involved," he repeated.

"Be there, " said the priest, ignoring Mad Tom's protestations. Father Funge rose from the stool. "God keep you well, now. Goodnight."

There was an awkward silence. Mad Tom knew the priest wanted a lift home but there was no way he was venturing out into that fearsome moonlight.

"I'd love to give you a lift home, Father, but poor Capall's right foot is a bit lame. It needs to rest."

Father Funge put on his biretta. Mad Tom opened the door and watched him walk out into the chilly night.

The young girl hurried home. She knew her father would be furious with her for being so late. He might even take his leather belt to her. Her mother would say how sick with worry she was, especially with the recent murders.

Cáit hadn't meant to stay so long in Mairéad's house, but they were working on a quilt for Mairéad's sister who was getting married in December. It was a surprise, and they could only work on it when she was not there in the cottage, or when she was asleep.

Cáit knew Mairéad's sister would love it. It was amazing what could be achieved from a few scraps of coloured material. Cáit was asked to assist for she was the best at sewing. Mairéad's mother even said so, and she could make anything from a child's dress to a man's shirt.

Cáit could see the dim light of the farm off in the distance. Maybe her father was out in the local tavern; she sincerely hoped so. Perhaps her mother was asleep. She might be able to sneak in without anyone seeing her. She only hoped the farm dog wouldn't start barking.

As she got closer to the big horse chestnut tree with its inky branches that webbed out across the night sky, she thought she saw something move among the branches. This panicked Cáit until she realised it was only a barn owl. It glided down silently and veered away, ghosting over the fields.

There was a small copse up ahead which she hated passing in the dark; it was supposed to be haunted ever since a neighbour hanged himself there. Her eyes were wild with fear, her heart pounding in her chest. There might be something horrible in the shadows waiting to attack at any minute. Keeping her eyes straight ahead she ran past the tall sentinel trees, then climbed over the wooden gate and out into the clear fields, finally reaching the cottage.

She gave a deep sigh of relief and looked back to make sure nothing was lurking in the shadows. All was quiet. Sneaking in the back door of the cottage, she could see her mother asleep on the chair beside the warm turf fire. She tiptoed into her room. Her younger sister lay sound asleep in the other bed. She quickly removed her clothes and got into her night shirt.

Her heart was still pounding. She tried to relax, hoping that her father would be safe coming home those lonely roads after all the recent killings. A light rain began to beat at the bedroom window.

At the edge of the copse a shadow seemed to pull away from the tree and become a moving shape.

From the canopy of the elm trees an explosion of dark wings curled and reeled in frenzied flight, cawing and crying until they finally moved away over the fields. Cáit sat up with a start, wondering what could have disturbed the rooks while they were sleeping. After a time, things became quiet again. Cáit settled down to sleep.

A misty fog began to seep in through the cracks of the bedroom window, forming itself into a man. Cáit felt eyes were watching her in the darkness. She opened her eyes to see a tall, handsome stranger standing at the end of her bed. She wanted to scream out, but her voice would not respond to the command.

He had taken her hand before she realised it and pulled her towards him.

She looked into his fiery red eyes and began to feel dizzy. He smiled a cold smile. She could see sharp fangs protruding from his mouth. His other hand moved around the back of her head and he pulled her closer, then he swiftly bit into her neck.

Father Funge was awakened in the early hours of the

morning by heavy pounding on the door. When he opened it, a very distraught Matt Walsh stood there shaking all over, almost unable to relate the death of his poor daughter Cáit.

When Father Funge and the man arrived at the cottage, Mrs Walsh and her younger daughter Christine were standing in silent vigil over the body of Cáit. Father Funge gazed at the terrible sight. Cáit's neck was smeared with blood. Rivulets of blood had spilled down on to the white sheets. He nervously examined her neck more closely.

"What monster could have done this?" Mrs Walsh begged for an answer.

Father Funge had a lost look in his eyes. He had no answer. He only knew that this killing was slightly different from the others he had seen. They'd had their throats torn open. The young girl's throat had two deep puncture marks and purple bruising along the neck.

Father Funge said some prayers over the body and left, promising he would return the next day.

# Chapter Seven

Mad Tom stopped at the blacksmith's forge. "Are you there, Benji?"

The blacksmith emerged from around the side of the forge. Mad Tom jumped back. There was a frightened look in his eyes.

"You're very jumpy, what's the matter?"

"Nothing," Mad Tom grunted. "Will you ever check Capall's shoes? I think they need replacing." Benji lifted up the front leg of the horse. "By God, they're in need of repair all right."

"Can I have a drink?" asked Mad Tom.

"Sure, go on into the house."

"From the trough will do me," he grinned. "Plenty of iron in that water, good for ye! My old grandfather used to swear by it. Good for the kidneys, the gums, the teeth."

"Rather you than me," said Benji.

"You see, you don't know what's good for you," said Mad Tom. He drank down over a pint of water.

"No wonder they call you 'Mad'," said the blacksmith.

Mad Tom moved closed to him and prodded him with

his finger. "I never suffer from toothache because of that water. So I'm mad in the right direction."

"Well, I'll stick to my well of crystal-pure water."

"When will you have the horse ready? You see, I have to go visit Father Funge about something very important, he needs my help."

"He must need more than *your* help."

"What do you mean?" Mad Tom enquired.

"He wants me and a few others as well. I was just on my way when you called."

Mad Tom scratched his face. "Sure, we'll head over together. You can fix Capall up later."

When they arrived at the priest's house, Mad Tom recognised the two men who were at The Madra Rua near Kilmore Quay the night the young couple were killed.

"Thanks for coming," said a grim-faced Father Funge. He introduced them to each other, then told them about the killing of the young girl. The blood drained from Mad Tom's face when he heard the priest relate the ghastly events.

"I know there's wickedness in the world," said the priest. "I've seen my fair share of it. But this . . . I have never seen the likes of it before. I don't know why, but I have a gut feeling that it has something to do with the night *The Dark Star* hit the rocks and a stranger survived. I said this to Tom here only last night."

Mad Tom nodded in agreement.

"Now, and more than ever since the death of young Cáit last night, I'm convinced there's a connection." There was a long silence, then the priest said firmly, "I have called you all here today to help me track down this stranger. No one has seen the stranger and lived," said the priest, "except Tom here."

Tom shuffled nervously from one position to another.

"I have asked in every tavern and inn from here to Wexford town but no one has seen or heard of him." Then, turning to Mad Tom, he asked him to relate all that had happened since he'd encountered this stranger. Mad Tom's eyes locked in contact with the priest's. They stared hard at each other.

Suddenly the door to the room opened, breaking the tension of the moment and startling Mad Tom. "It's only dear Miss Cloney with some welcome refreshments." The old woman placed a tray on a table. Mad Tom's eyes widened, looking at all the delicious cake and soda bread on offer. "Thank you, Nan," said Father Funge as he closed the door after the woman.

The men helped themselves to tea and cake. They all relaxed, then Mad Tom related his encounters with the foreigner, giving a detailed account of their first meeting, up to the burial of the six coffins. "Well, they were more like crates," he added, as he scoffed some more cake. The others listened in silence.

The priest put down his mug and said he did not know whether they were dealing with some bloodthirsty madman or the devil himself.

Jacko reached over for some soda bread, then looked up at the others. "Have you ever heard of a Nosferatu?"

"A what?" asked Timmy.

"A vampire," said Jacko. "A bloodsucker."

There was no reply.

"Please continue," said Father Funge.

"Well, I have travelled the seven seas and have seen the strangest of things and heard the wildest of stories. But a few years ago, oh, it must be seven by now, I was staying on a Greek island called Crete. During my sojourn there, in a small place called Sitia at the eastern end of the island, a number of handsome young men from the village were killed, their throats torn open. The villagers in Sitia thought it was some kind of a wild beast. They searched the hills and shot and killed any wild creature they could see, but the killing continued.

"Then, one evening, a shepherd passing by an old cemetery saw a beautiful young woman walking through the grounds with what he took to be her lover. Shortly afterwards, there was a terrible scream. The old shepherd hurried to the village and told the villagers what he had witnessed. A large group followed him back to the cemetery and there they found a dead man with a young woman lying over him, feeding from him like a leech. They could not catch her for she had the strength of ten men. She had two pointed fangs as big as a wolf's. She growled and hissed then vanished in a puff of smoke. They had all recognised the young woman. She had recently returned to the island after living abroad for several years. They managed to track her down with some hunting dogs. She was sleeping in a crypt during the daylight hours."

Jacko finished the soda bread, then drank some tea.

"Well, what happened then?" asked Mad Tom.

"They had brought with them a sharp wooden stake

and some garlic. They hammered the stake into her demon heart. That's the only way to dispatch a vampire," he added. "Only then did they know they had finally destroyed her, for she was already dead, 'the undead' as they're called. They put the garlic in her mouth. The old priest of the island explained the ritual and that it was the only way to free her soul."

"What a story," said Timmy. "That would give me the creeps."

"What happened to the young men? Were they infected?" asked Benji.

"No, it seemed she didn't want to make new vampires, she only wanted to feed on them. But all the victims of the vampire were staked just in case," said Jacko.

"Nosferatu," said the priest. Then, turning to Jacko, he continued, "I think you may have hit the nail on the head. It must be one of those undead creatures we are dealing with."

"Can I go now?" asked Mad Tom. " I have a lot to do."

The priest ignored his plea. "I have asked you strong men here today to help me find this monster. And, if what Jacko says is true, we need to work during the daylight hours, for it would appear that these vampire creatures need to rest during God's daylight."

"You can count me out," said Mad Tom. "I've told you all I know – I don't want a bloodthirsty fiend on the scent of my blood, thank you very much."

"Would you stand by and see another innocent fall victim to this devil?"

"Everyone has to look out for themselves in this world,

no one is going to do it for you." Mad Tom headed for the door.

Benji the blacksmith barred the way. "Listen, Tom, we all know how you feel . . . but I've two daughters of my own and I don't want them put at risk if we can prevent it. It's our God-given duty to do it."

Mad Tom knew he hadn't much choice. Benji was the strongest man in Fethard and the surrounding area, perhaps the whole county. "OK, I'll help whatever way I can, but I expect Capall to be shod free."

Benji put out his hand and offered it to Tom. "It's a deal."

"I hate to mention this, but I think that young girl who was killed last night could run the risk of becoming a vampire," Jacko added gravely.

"We've no time to lose," said the priest. "Let us go to the Walsh's as soon as the horse is ready."

It was late afternoon when they arrived at the Walsh's farm. Most of the locals were there and the keeners. Matt Walsh and his wife Mairéad stood silently by. Their youngest daughter was weeping by the bedside along with her friends.

"God save you all," said Father Funge.

"Thank you for coming," said Mrs Walsh.

Father Funge took her firmly by the hand. "Can we talk outside?" he asked.

Matt and Mairéad seemed surprised at his request. As they went outside, they saw the other men standing around awkwardly.

"Sorry for your troubles," said Benji, wringing his cap with his big hands.

Mairéad nodded in gratitude. "Would you be wanting tea?" asked Matt.

"No need to ask," said Mairéad. "I'll put fresh water on right away."

"No, no. We have something we feel we must tell you." Father Funge found it difficult to find the words to explain what they wanted to do.

When he finally managed to convey why they had come, Matt Walsh stood in front of Father Funge. "No one is going to harm a hair on my daughter's head. Do you all hear what I'm saying? She is going to rest in peace."

Mairead pulled her husband back by the arm. "Is it true what you have told us, that this creature who killed my poor daughter has the power over her even in death?"

"God help me, but I believe it's the truth and she could end up like this vile thing herself, doomed to walk the earth feeding on human blood." Father Funge turned away. He couldn't bear to look at the grief in Mairéad's eyes as they began to fill up again with tears.

She turned to her husband. "Go. Fetch a hazel branch and put a sharp point on one end, like the priest suggested." Mairéad asked all the mourners to leave, saying she would see them the next day at the funeral. They were surprised at the request but they left, one by one. "You too, daughter, you go. Stay with your friends and come back before dark."

Matt Walsh returned with the pointed hazel stick. He

handed it to the priest. "You do it, Father. I won't pierce my own daughter's heart. I couldn't."

Father Funge reluctantly took the stake and entered the bedroom. With trembling hands, he held it over the dead girl's chest. He said a few silent prayers then raised his arms higher. As he gazed on the sweet form, he trembled even more. He couldn't bring himself to drive the stake in. "God forgive me," he wept bitterly. "I cannot do it either." He staggered away from the corpse.

"Give it to me," said Jacko. "I'll do it."

"No," said Mairéad, as she took the stake from the priest. "I brought this dear child into the world. I've nursed her and watched her grow strong and tall. She was always a good daughter, and if freeing her eternal soul means driving this wooden stake through her I will, with the grace of God. Go into the other room and leave me for a few moments alone with her."

Matt Walsh automatically threw a few more sods on the fire and hung the kettle over it. There was an eerie silence as they waited for Mairead to do the terrible deed. Suddenly they heard Mairéad cry out and they knew the stake had entered the body. This was followed by an unearthly scream, then a groan.

Matt Walsh looked at the priest in horror. "That was my darling Cáit screaming."

"I know, I know," said Father Funge sadly.

Mairéad entered from the bedroom in a trance-like state. Wiping her bloodstained hands on a cloth, she said quietly, "It is done. My darling child is set free."

# Chapter Eight

Doyler sat in his battered red Hiace van outside the Gresham Hotel. He checked his watch. It was twenty to seven. He was waiting for Cooley, who had just popped out to get some fish and chips for them. He checked the rear-view mirror and watched him turning up the street. Cooley opened the van door. Doyler immediately caught the smell of the chips

"Aah," he sighed with pleasure. "You can't beat the smell of chips drowned in vinegar." Then he took the brown grease-stained bag and rummaged through it. "I hope you got me ray and chips, I specifically asked for ray and chips. This looks like cod."

"Keep your hair on," said Cooley. "The ray is under the cod, and I got large chips." They relaxed and sat back and began to eat the food. "Isn't Dublin grand when all the shoppers are gone home? Things are nice and peaceful. The city belongs to the pigeons again." Doyler gave him a sarcastic look. "I just had a thought," said Cooley.

"What do you want, a medal?" snapped Doyler.

"No, listen," insisted Cooley. "I hope that doctor fella

has the sense to hire a car. I don't suppose he'd fancy a trip to Wexford in this heap of junk."

"I never thought of that. We never discussed whether we were to drive him there or not."

"What time is it now?"

"It's five to seven," said Doyler.

"God, I was starvin'," said Cooley, as he wiped his mouth with his sleeve.

"I don't know where you put it," said Doyler. "You're as thin as a rake."

"Ah, you can't fatten a thoroughbred," Cooley retorted.

A sudden loud tap on the glass gave them both a start. It was a Garda. "You can't park this vehicle here. You'll have to move."

Cooley rolled down the window. "We're waiting for someone, Miss. Or, I mean, Guard."

"You've been parked there over ten minutes, now move along."

Doyler started up the engine, stuck his arm out the window to indicate he was pulling out, then drove away. "I'll just drive around the block," he growled.

"The women are getting as bad as the men," said Cooley.

"Put them into uniform and they become Saddam Husseins."

As they approached the Gresham Hotel again, they noticed a pearl-grey Audi parked with hazard lights flashing.

"I think that's him," said Cooley. They pulled up

behind. Cooley checked that the Garda was gone. "Good evening, Doctor. A grand evening for a drive."

"Follow me," said Doctor Drachler.

"Do you know the way?" asked Cooley.

"I have a map. We'll stop for coffee in Gorey." The doctor pulled out and sped away.

"Follow him," said Cooley to Doyler.

"Well, what else do you think I would do?" snapped Doyler.

"I would have gone the other road myself, but he wants us to stop for coffee in Gorey then go on into Wexford town."

"Well, he's paying, so that's fine. We can go through Limerick for all I care as long as he's paying the expenses." They both laughed loudly.

When they arrived at Gorey, the doctor flashed them down.

"Traffic was light," said Cooley.

Doctor Drachler put the alarm on his car. "I will meet you there." He pointed to a nice coffee shop along the main street. "Order me a coffee, I will be along soon." They watched him walk up along the street and stop at a pet shop.

"What's he doing?" asked Cooley.

"How would I know? But no pet shop is going to be open at eight-thirty on a Saturday evening, that's for certain. Let's go in, it's getting nippy out here."

Doctor Drachler arrived in with a wicker basket, sat down alongside them and put the basket under the table. Cooley and Doyler stared in amazement but didn't want to ask what was in the basket. The doctor poured himself black coffee from the stainless steel pot.

Sensing their curiosity he said, "It's a cat, a present for someone."

"Oh, very nice," said Cooley. "I hate cats myself."

Doyler kicked him under the table, then he piped up, "Cats are grand. I don't have one myself but I always put out a saucer of milk for the neighbour's cat."

"Tell me about this abbey we are going to?"

Doyler was completely taken unawares with the question. "You mean its history?" The doctor nodded. "Well, it's very old . . ." Doyler began, struggling to find something to say about it.

"It was founded around 1200 AD," said Cooley, "by William Earl Marshall, for the Cistercians. It was named after Tintern de Voto in Wales. I think Marshall was married to Strongbow's daughter. There was extensive building carried out in the 15th century – the tower was built then. Elizabeth I granted it to Anthony Colclough in 1566. He's buried there in the chapel of the abbey. Then in 1641, the abbey was attacked by the native Irish. By the 19th century the Colclough family was residing in the former nave of the abbey. Their descendents lived there up to the 1960s even though the place was almost in ruins." Cooley looked at the doctor and Doyler, and could see he had a captive audience. "After that, when it was no longer inhabited, it became very neglected. In 1982, the Office of Public Works, a government organisation, "began to restore the abbey and the work is still in progress. It has a chancel, nave, tower and vaulted chapels. There is a wood around the area and Coillte have planted new trees there."

"I'm very impressed with your knowledge of the abbey," said the doctor. He finished his coffee, then excused himself and headed towards the toilet.

"Did you swallow the *Encyclopaedia Britannica* or what, Cooley? There's a nave, a tower and vaulted chapels . . ." Doyler mimicked Cooley.

"Ah, you're just jealous," said Cooley. Doyler blew his nose in annoyance. "To tell you the truth, I picked up a few leaflets from the Government Buildings and read up on it this morning."

"Smart move," said Doyler. "It's important these foreigners realise they're not dealing with muck here."

A red BMW drove slowly up the street.

"There," said Peter excitedly. "That's the van."

"Well done," said Dermod. They pulled in on the other side of the street and waited. "I'm delighted you could come," said Dermod to Amanda.

"When Vinny told me what you were doing, I said I'd come along for the ride."

"Of course, it's nothing to do with the fact that her boyfriend stood her up again."

"You shut up," said Amanda; then, feeling a little embarrassed, she explained to Dermod how her boyfriend worked in a local pub and had been asked to work overtime because of the big match this weekend. "To be honest, I'm getting a bit fed up with it. I'm working all day and he's working all night."

"I know the feeling," said Dermod. "I was in a serious relationship for over five years. My ex-girlfriend was an animator. When we were broke and out of work, we were always together. Then we both became extremely busy. She got to work on some big animation movies but it meant she had to move to California. I ended up working on some big projects in Boston. We officially split up last summer. It was the pressure of work, really. Oh, we still keep in touch with an occasional humorous letter full of quirky doodles," Dermod sighed.

"Maybe you'll get back together," said Amanda.

"No, I don't think so. From her last correspondence, it seems she has met someone else. A producer!" There was an awkward silence.

"I'm starving," said Gary. "Can we get chips?"

Julie piped up. "Didn't Dermod buy us all burgers and chips earlier?"

Dermod turned around to listen. "We'll get some more chips on the way home . . . and if we do see any vampires, we'll get double chips," he smiled broadly.

"We'll need steaks as well," said Peter. "Get it? Stakes!"

"Yes, we get it," said Vinny. "Very funny."

"Look," said Julie. They're coming out of the café."

Doyler and Cooley got into the van. The doctor placed the wicker basket in the boot of the car and, in a couple of seconds, they were away down the street and, turning left, on their way to Wexford town.

When they arrived, Doctor Drachler stopped at a dress hire and gentlemen's outfitters.

"What's he at now?" asked Doyler, pulling the van in alongside the car.

The doctor walked back to the van. "I will be only a couple of minutes."

"Right. We'll keep the engine running," grinned Doyler.

"What's he doing?" asked Cooley.

"I just asked the same question a moment ago, and the answer is I haven't the foggiest."

"Maybe he's dressing for supper," laughed Cooley.

"Here," said Doyler. "Hand me one of those Milky Moos." Doyler stuffed the sweet into his mouth and began to push it around inside his mouth. "I find chewing helps me relax when I get tense, and for some reason I'm getting more tense the nearer we get to this abbey."

"He's getting into the car again with a large cardboard box."

"How does he manage it?" said Doyler. "That shop was closed as well."

"Ah, money talks," said Cooley. "And opens doors." He elbowed Doyler. "Get my meaning?"

"Where now?" said Doyler.

"We turn before the petrol station and head for the ring of Hook. Just follow Doctor Drachler. He seems to know where he's going," said Cooley.

Doyler glanced in his rear-view mirror. "You know, I'm sure we're being followed by that red BMW behind us. I thought I saw it near the Gresham Hotel, then in Gorey it was parked on the main street. Now it's behind us."

Cooley looked around. "It's just a family, sure I can see the kids in the back of the car."

"Perhaps you're right," said Doyler. "After all, who would know what we're up to?"

"We don't even know ourselves," laughed Cooley.

In the half-light of gathering dusk the trees and reaching branches seemed to take on grotesque forms. Doyler scanned each side of the road. "Are we near this god-forsaken place, we're driving nearly half an hour?" he asked Cooley, who, since Wexford, was physically trembling in his seat.

The Audi, which was a good distance ahead, slowed almost to a stop. "He wants us to overtake now," said Cooley, "since I am the only one who knows the entrance." Doyler overtook the doctor and gave him a wave. "Slow," said Cooley. "It's near now. Yes, you see those two granite pillars? In through there . . ."

"God, this place looks spooky all right," said Doyler.

"Just follow the dirt road down to the abbey."

Something darted across the road. "What was that?" said Doyler.

"It was only a hare," said Cooley. "Relax."

"I'll relax when we're out of here with the few bob in our pockets and on the road to Dublin," snapped Doyler.

# Chapter Nine

November 18th 1861
Tintern Abbey, County Wexford.

As they made their way down the dirt-track towards the abbey, Mad Tom could sense the horse's fear. Her nose was lifted skywards and her ears were laid flat back. She was tossing her head up and down and sideways, and she gave out a rattling whinny. "What is it, Capall?" asked Mad Tom as he gave her more rein.

"You are sure the Colclough family is abroad?" enquired Father Funge.

"Yes," said Mad Tom. "America, I think. Servants and all are away. They're not expected back until the New Year."

"How do you know?" asked Benji.

"I know," said Mad Tom, "because a poacher friend of mine keeps me up to date with everything that goes on around these parts."

They arrived at the front gate of the abbey. The place was deserted, boarded up. The five men got down from the cart with shovels and spades. The priest carried a large, black leather bag. They moved slowly along the abbey wall over towards the cemetery. It was early afternoon; a chilly wind blew up from the estuary. A grey heron flapped overhead, making them cower.

"We're all becoming jumpy," said the priest.

They watched its deliberate, slow wingbeats as it headed down to the mudflats. A flock of dunlin could be seen rising from the estuary, having mistaken the heron for a bird of prey. They circled the grey sky then returned to feeding on the mudflats.

Finally they arrived at the small cemetery. Mad Tom kicked at the ground; a small sod lifted up. "Well, at least the ground is not too hard. Must be because of all the rain we had earlier in the week."

They looked at all the old tombstones, then the priest turned to Tom. "Well, where did you bury them?"

"Over there, beyond that yew tree."

"We'd better get on with it." They each took turns to dig out some clay. The sweat began to pour off them as they dug deeper and deeper.

Finally, Benji hit something firm. "I think I've found one." A few more shovels of clay revealed the long wooden crate.

Mad Tom stepped back as Benji prised the lid open. "Good God!" exclaimed Benji. "It's filled with soil."

"I thought you said he was bringing his ancestors in these coffins," snapped the priest.

"That's what he told me," said Mad Tom.

Jacko touched the priest on the arm. "It's his native soil. A vampire has to rest on his native soil."

"Let's get out of here," pleaded Mad Tom.

"No," said the priest. "We'll finish what we set out to do." The priest put a crucifix on the soil, then sprinkled holy water over it all. "That will put an end to him resting here," the priest said in defiance.

Timmy said they should hurry as the light was beginning to go. They dug and dug frantically, searching for the other crates. Heaving and panting they managed to locate four more. The priest quickly placed a crucifix or holy relic on the soil and sprinkled them all over with holy water. "Where is the last one?" asked the priest. "You said there were six."

"I don't know," said Mad Tom. "The stranger buried some himself. I think it was over there . . ." Mad Tom frantically scrambled around to find the other spot. Then he stepped back in horror. "It was buried there." He pointed to a newly-dug hole, but not one that they just had dug.

"Are you sure?" cried Benji.

"Yes, I'm telling you it was buried here," Mad Tom stammered. "It's gone. Someone's taken it!"

The priest thought for a minute. "He must have moved it, probably placed it in one of the vaults of the old abbey."

"We'd better find it," said Jacko, "before it gets too dark."

They hurried back to the abbey, climbed over a shattered wall, and arrived in the courtyard. "Over there," said Timmy, pointing to steps which led underground.

Mad Tom held on to the spade like a weapon. Opening his black bag, the priest removed a storm lantern then went rummaging for a flint box. Jacko produced one from his coat pocket and, within seconds, the lamp was lit.

A chill of apprehension came over them as they descended the stairs. The air was damp and cold. The musty odour almost made Father Funge retch.

"Are you all right?" asked Benji.

"Fine. Let's get this over with."

Deeper and deeper down into the bowels of the abbey they went, moving more cautiously than ever, full of fear and trepidation. A mass of tangled cobwebs brushed off their faces, then a flurry of black wings flapped by them. Mad Tom could not control the hysterical scream that echoed around the vaults.

"It's only bats," said Jacko, trying to reassure him. "Probably roosting here for the winter."

"Those bats nearly gave me a heart attack," Mad Tom grunted.

On and on they moved until they reached a heavy oaken door, bolted from the outside. They looked at each other in silence. They had no idea what lay behind the door; they could only hope that, if it was a vampire, it was sleeping.

The priest nodded to Benji, who took a firm grip on the rusty bolt and pulled it open. He pushed at the door. It did not move. Putting his shoulder to it, he pushed with all his might. The rusty hinges screeched loudly as the door swung open. Holding the lantern up ahead of them, they passed through. Father Funge led the way with the storm lamp held high above his head. Rats scurried around their feet, causing them all to recoil and scream out.

Then they saw the crate. It had been placed on top of a

marble tomb. "Dear God, there it is," said Mad Tom. They were all trembling as they watched Benji begin to prise off the lid. He stepped back and gestured to the others to come closer.

Father Funge peered in. A beautiful ebony coffin with golden handles rested inside the crate. Father Funge put down the storm lantern and took out a mallet and a wooden stake. Beads of sweat poured down his face. He held the stake in his left hand and the mallet in his right, then nodded to Mad Tom and Benji to lift the lid up.

There the stranger lay, still as stone. Father Funge wrestled with his thoughts. It just didn't seem right to drive a stake through this handsome gentleman. Yet he knew it was no ordinary man but someone who preyed on others.

"Do it!" Jacko called out.

Father Funge placed the point of the stake just above the stranger's chest and held the mallet high, ready to drive it into the black-hearted fiend. In an instant, the stranger opened his eyes. They were red as flaming coals. There was a look of intense hatred on his face as he spread his lips, revealing two deadly fangs. He snarled like a wolf. Father Funge recoiled in horror, dropping the stake and mallet. Mad Tom and Timmy rushed to escape out the passageway.

"Let's get out of here!" yelled Benji to Father Funge, who seemed rooted to the spot. Benji grabbed him and the storm lantern. "Let's go." Benji pulled him away and out the doorway.

Jacko picked up the mallet and stake. "But the job's

not finished!" he shouted after the others, as he watched them escape along the tunnel. He moved over to the coffin, determined to put an end to this vampire once and for all. "No! No!" he yelled in the faded light, for when he reached into the coffin the vampire was gone. But how? Where? He looked around in the poor light and saw him standing in the shadows.

"You fool," said the vampire. "Did you think you could so easily destroy me? I have lived for over four centuries."

Jacko slowly backed away towards the door. "Damn you, devil," he shouted, throwing the wooden mallet at the vampire. The vampire moved with lightning speed to avoid the object, then snarled and flashed his deadly fangs.

Groping and clawing his way along the tunnel, Mad Tom was the first to reach the stairs and the first to climb up them, followed by Timmy, their hearts pounding in their chests. "Let's get out of this place!

"What about the others?" asked Timmy. "We can't leave them," he yelled, pulling at the sleeve of Tom's coat.

"We can't stay here to be torn to pieces by that bloodsucker."

Just then Father Funge and Benji arrived, panting hard.

"Where's ol Jacko?" Timmy asked.

"He wanted to stay and finish what we set out to do," said Benji.

"We can't leave him," Timmy pleaded.

"You're right," said the priest.

"It's almost night," said Mad Tom. "We won't stand a chance if we hang around here."

Suddenly there was a loud piercing cry. A terrible fear swept over them, for they all knew it was from poor Jacko. "He's done for," said Benji. "Mad Tom is right, we'd better get away from here." They scrambled over the wall and ran like crazy to where the horse and cart were.

Capall was rearing and stamping her feet like a creature possessed. Mad Tom untied the reins and leapt on to the cart, pulling away from where he had tied her up. The others barely had time to climb aboard. Soon they were away down the dirt-track, heading for home.

It was late evening before Mad Tom finally reached his cottage, having left the priest and Benji home first. His horse was in a lather of sweat. She was frothing at the mouth. Mad Tom quickly undid the cart and untied the reins.

"Thank you, my beauty, for getting me out of that place." He quickly filled a bucket and left it for her. "Don't go drinking it all at once," he said to her, then hurried into the cottage. He bolted all the doors and windows, lit a lamp and took out a bottle of brandy, then picked up the sword and placed it on the table. "If that priest thinks I'm going back tomorrow, he's out of his mind," he said, picking up one of the cats and stroking it gently. "They had their chance tonight to get rid of the bloodsucker, but they blew it. Now they want to melt down the silver crucifixes from the church and make a silver band to wrap around the coffin. Benji said that would seal the vampire in forever. The priest is prepared to go along with it. Well, they can do what they like. I want no part of it. Even that chap Timmy thought it was mad to return there. He said he was getting on the first ship out of Wexford. He didn't care where it was bound for."

Mad Tom would have loved to do the same, but he had a lot of booty collected over the years. He couldn't afford to take it – nor could he afford to leave it behind.

Perhaps the vampire would clear off now that his hiding-place had been discovered. Mad Tom sincerely hoped so, though he didn't wish the creature on any other folk either. Mad Tom was not going to leave his cottage for the next few weeks. He had enough supplies; he was just going to sit tight.

Timmy had persuaded Bridie, the innkeeper's wife in The Madra Rua, to give him a room for the night. She gladly agreed after she heard what had happened to his poor friend, Jacko. Every crucifix and holy relic that could be found was placed over the doors and windows of the inn, for fear the creature might come calling.

Timmy was shown to the loft bedroom by the innkeeper. He thanked him and settled in for the night. Bolting the bedroom door, he began to feel a little more relaxed. He thought the priest and blacksmith were very brave, wanting to return to the Abbey. He hadn't the courage to join them, not after what happened to old Jacko. The silver band might do the trick and stop this vampire – he wished them luck.

He stretched out on the bed and kicked off his boots. "After breakfast, I'm off." That was a promise he'd made to himself and he planned to keep it.

A large bat flapped across the night sky and alighted on the roof of The Madra Rua. Under the chilly starry night, a transformation was taking place in the shadows. Now the stranger stood where the bat had alighted. Swiftly, silently he moved over towards the loft window with the grace of an animal. There was still light behind the small curtains. Suddenly there was the sound of breaking glass. Timmy stared in terror as the vampire came through the window.

A clock chimed midnight.

Mad Tom fingered the beautiful golden watch, the one he'd found in the rock pool after the shipwreck. It didn't work then, but when it dried out it began to work beautifully. He wound it, then said to the cat that it was time for bed. He stood up and stretched. A truly dreadful day, he thought to himself, one he knew he would never forget.

*. . . his long black cloak billowing around . . .*

He picked up the sword and placed it beside his bed. Sitting down on the edge, he began to remove his boots. Outside, the mare whinnied loudly, then he heard her galloping in the dark across the fields. "What the devil!" he exclaimed. The cats began to hiss, their fur standing on end.

Mad Tom moved over to the window. A feeling of dread came over him as he peered out into the darkness. There was nothing unusual to be seen. Picking up the sword, he went into the other room and peered out that window. A cry of horror rose from him. Just outside the cottage door he could see the stranger standing, his long black cloak billowing around – shrouding his body.

Mad Tom quickly pulled the table in front of the door and wedged a chair on top of it. "Keep away," he yelled, holding the sword towards the door. "It wasn't my idea – I never wanted to go to the abbey. They made me do it!" There was an ominous silence. Mad Tom knew there was no place to hide and stood trembling, expecting the worst.

For several moments nothing happened, then the table began to move and the chair fell to the ground. The bolts of the door seemed to spring free on their own. Mad Tom was rooted to the spot. Before he knew what was happening, the stranger stood menacingly before him, his body framed by moonlight – then he appeared to almost float into the room, for in an instant he was only a few feet away from Mad Tom, who was still holding the sword.

An evil smile broke across the stranger's face. "What is that for?" he asked, gesturing to the sword. "Planning to use it on someone?"

"You . . . you devil, if you come any closer," he waved the sword slightly, "I swear to God, I'll run you through."

"That's not very friendly," said the stranger. "And to think how well we got on when first we met."

Mad Tom held his position as the stranger attempted to move closer. "Stay back!" he warned.

"Did you know that to make such a beautiful sword they have to heat the metal almost to melting-point? Then it can be moulded to the will of the craftsman, or should I say blacksmith?"

Mad Tom could not believe his eyes as he watched the point of the sword become red-hot. The heat quickly spread up towards the hilt. Tom could feel his hands getting hotter and hotter. The pain became unbearable as the full heat reached the handle. Mad Tom screamed with pain as he tried to keep a grip on the sword. Finally, the pain was too much to bear. He opened up his hands and the sword went crashing to the ground. Mad Tom held his blistering hands up to his face in disbelief.

"You'd better sit down," said the stranger. Suddenly a terrible force sent Mad Tom flying across the room, crashing down on to a chair. Mad Tom hugged himself with his blistered hands and began to rock to and fro. "One learns a few tricks over the centuries," the stranger grinned. "Now perhaps you will tell me what other surprises your friends are planning?" Mad Tom sat and stared hard back at him. "By the way, your little band of heroes has been reduced to three, including you, of course." Mad Tom's expression changed as he wondered who it was. "I suppose I should put you out of your misery, for I know you must be wondering on whom I came calling. It was the thin one with the curly black hair, I never did get his name . . . he tried to outwit me by staying in a different place tonight. No one can hide from me. I caught up with him in a tavern, hiding in the loft." Mad Tom knew immediately it was Timmy. "I hope he wasn't a close friend of yours . . ." the stranger said in mock sympathy.

"No, but he was a likeable young fella," said Tom sadly.

"You still haven't told me what the other two are planning, or if they have been sharing their little adventure with other townsfolk."

"Why don't you ask them yourself? I'll tell you nothing, only curse you to hell."

"It's a pity you are taking such a severe approach, but I admire the bit of courage you have shown, however miniscule. Now, before I leave, I will show you one more trick. Watch carefully, for I wouldn't want you to miss the point of it. Nothing up my sleeves!" He gestured with each hand to the opposite arm. Then, placing his right hand a few feet over the sword, he drew the sword from the floor as if his hand were a magnet, leaving it suspended in midair in a horizontal position with the point facing Tom. "This is what is called 'mind over matter'. Clever, don't you think? But that's not the whole trick," he grinned. "Watch carefully."

Tom screamed as the sword cut through the air like an arrow heading straight for him. Mad Tom felt a sharp piercing pain as the sword tore into his chest. A moment later his head slumped down, his body pinned to the wall.

The stranger pulled one of the cats from its hiding-place and stroked it. "See? Nothing to be afraid of."

# Chapter Ten

The beams from the torches pierced the darkness as Doyler and Cooley scanned the courtyard for the entrance to the vaults.

"This place gives me the willies," said Cooley.

"Shut up," said Doyler. "We don't want yer man to think we're afraid of the dark."

Doctor Drachler gestured to them. "It's over here," he said, pointing to the steps.

"After you," said Doyler.

Doctor Drachler took the torch from him and headed down the steps.

Cooley was holding the wicker basket with the cat inside and the large cardboard box. "You take my torch. I can barely manage these."

"Stop complaining. We're going to be well paid for it."

"I know," said Cooley. "You keep telling me."

"Well, just remember it and follow me down these steps. Mind yourself, some of them are very slippery. We don't want to break our necks before we get the loot." They could see the black form of Doctor Drachler up ahead. Curtains of cobwebs stretched from wall to wall.

Doctor Drachler brushed them aside as he moved along the tunnel. He stopped before a heavy wooden door where he was joined by Doyler and Cooley.

"No one has been down here for a long time," Cooley remarked.

Shining the torch on the rusty bolt, Doctor Drachler gestured to the others to pull it across. Doyler spat on his hands and wrestled with the bolt, up and down, until it moved freely, then he slid it across. They tried to push the door open but it did not budge. Cooley and Doyler pushed with all their might and, eventually, the rusty hinges snapped and the heavy oaken door fell in, sending Doyler and Cooley crashing down on top of it.

"Get off me," said Doyler as he pushed Cooley away.

"Aah," yelled Cooley. "Look! There!"

Doctor Drachler's torch beam moved to the spot where Cooley was pointing. It was a human skeleton lying across the floor.

"Well, what would you expect to find in a crypt?" said Doyler, pretending not to be startled, but he was just as much afraid as his friend. Doyler and Cooley got up and dusted themselves off. "Probably the remains of the last monk that lived here," said Doyler. "Came down to die alongside the others but never managed to reach the tomb. Just keeled over here."

"I reckon it's more recent than that," said Cooley, elbowing Doyler. Cooley searched the floor with the beam. "Look over there!" He shone the torch at a piece of wood. "That looks like a stake to me! I reckon we've found our authentic vampire. It all adds up," he said in excited tones. "The vampire hunters came here, staked the creature while it lay sleeping, then they quickly made a run for it. The vampire staggered from its resting-place trying to make it to the door, at the same time pulling out the stake and throwing it there. It reached the door but was too weak to open it. It collapsed and died."

"Brilliant," said Doyler. "I mean, I agree with you completely. There wouldn't be any other explanation. Let's put the skeleton in a bag with this wooden stake and get out of here before anyone sees us."

"Not so fast," said the doctor, who was standing in the centre of the room. He was shining his torchlight over a timber crate that was on the floor beside a marble tomb. Doyler and Cooley nervously moved over to it. "Open it up," demanded the doctor. "Carefully," he added.

"Well, go ahead," said Doyler shining his torch beam on Cooley's face as if to see his expression of fear and protest.

Cooley swallowed hard and began to lever off the lid. A large piece broke away like damp cardboard.

"This crate is rotten!" said Doyler, kicking a large hole in the side of it where his boot made contact. The whole crate collapsed in on itself. A cloud of dust lifted, making Cooley, who was the closest to it, sneeze and cough. When he recovered Cooley said authoritatively, "That must have been the box where the vampire slept. Over the years it was eaten away by woodworm, mildew and rising damp."

"Pity," said Doyler. "It would have been handy to keep it had it been in decent nick. We could have placed the skeleton in it and wired the wooden stake on to the ribcage. Still, we could always get a mate to knock up another crate and age it a bit. No one could tell the difference." Doyler sensed the doctor's look of contempt. "Well, what I mean is, everything else is genuine. Nowadays, people love a bit of show biz and razzmatazz, it adds to the spectacle." Suddenly there was a sharp squeal. "What was that?" Doyler was becoming panicky.

"Sorry," said Cooley. "I must have stepped on a rat."

"Come here, the two of you," said Doctor Drachler. "I need you to move this lid with me." Placing the torches carefully on another tomb that the maximum light would shine on the marble tomb, Cooley hurried over to help them.

"A very fancy tomb for a monk," remarked Doyler.

"It's a knight's tomb, actually," said Cooley.

"Just push!" said Doyler. "And don't be such a know-all." The marble lid refused to budge. "It's mighty stiff," he said.

"We'll try lifting and sliding," the doctor suggested.

"Move, ye boyo!" said Cooley as they all gripped one corner of the lid. Prising it up a little, the marble surface groaned and the lid began slowly to slide across.

"Push harder," ordered the doctor.

They pushed with such force that the lid went sliding off the tomb, crashing to the floor and shattering into pieces. The doctor looked at the heavy fragments of marble strewn on the floor and let out a deep sigh of regret over the destruction of such a beautiful, ornate object.

Cooley picked up a torch and shone it into the tomb. "Aah," he gasped.

"What is it?" asked the doctor.

"Look for yourself," said Cooley, his voice trembling.

They all peered in at a beautiful ebony coffin with a tarnished band of silver around the centre of it. The doctor's eyes widened with delight. He felt sure he had found what he had been searching for for nearly forty years. An actual vampire's resting place! He wasn't sure what the silver band was for – there was no mention of it in the priest's journal. He suspected it must be some device to lock up for good what lay inside the coffin.

"We need to remove this silver strip. I have a hack-saw in the van," said Cooley. "I'll go and get it."

"Let me help you find it," said Doyler. "Be back in a jiffy."

The doctor sat on the wicker basket and wiped his face with his handkerchief. "Don't be long!" His voice was anxious.

Dermod looked out at the shroud of heavy mist creeping across the fields. "I think I should go and see what they're up to."

"Can I come?" asked Peter.

"No, you stay here," said Vinny.

"He's my uncle, not yours."

"Do you think it's wise?" asked Amanda.

"Don't worry," said Dermod. "I'm not about to do anything stupid. We've sat in this car for nearly an hour.

We're going to have to decide whether to stay overnight in Wexford or head back to Dublin."

"I don't mind either way," Amanda said warmly.

"And as for this lot, I don't think there'll be too much concern as long as they're with us." Dermod opened the door of the driver's side.

They could feel the blast of cool air rush in.

"That settles it," said Julie. "I'm staying here."

"Yes," said Dermod, looking protectively at Amanda. "I think it's wise if just Vinny and myself check out these shady characters."

Gary had fallen asleep in the back of the car. "He doesn't look too concerned," Amanda smiled.

"The dope stayed up until two this morning watching an Aliens video."

"Just lock the doors after us," insisted Dermod, as he and Vinny headed for the ruined abbey.

"Bring in that gas lamp as well," said Doyler. "The more light we have in that awful place, the better."

Cooley lit the gas lamp and got the hack-saw from underneath a blanket in the van. "Hey, Doyler? You don't suppose there is really a vampire in that coffin?"

"Not at all . . . probably some gimmick dreamed up by the locals to bring in tourists. They were up to all kinds of things in those days. Not much has changed when it comes to making mugs part with their money."

Cooley laughed. "You're probably right, although I got a bit of a bad vibe when . . ."

"Forget about your bad vibes and make sure that old

silver band isn't left behind. After a good clean-up, that'll be worth money. Come on, we'd better hurry back down. The sooner we get this business over with, the better."

"I don't know about you, but I'm freezing!" said Cooley.

"Listen, later we'll treat ourselves to big T-bone steaks, with garlic sauce and plenty of chips."

"Sounds great to me," said Cooley, following Doyler back to the vault.

"It looks very scary," said Vinny, as they observed the two men bathed in the pale light beside their van.

Dermod and Vinny watched them scramble over the broken wall, head across the courtyard and descend down some steps. The men appeared to be swallowed up by the darkness.

"Do you want a closer look?" asked Dermod.

"Why not?" said Vinny. "As long as you're here," he smiled. Then he added, "It's a deadly way to spend an evening."

"Let's go."

Quickly and quietly the two climbed over the wall and headed across the courtyard, keeping to the shadows until they arrived at the entrance to the vaults. Dermod produced a large penknife and snapped open the long blade. Vinny's eyes widened as he saw the blade glisten in the moonlight.

"I normally use this to sharpen my pencils," Dermod smiled. "But you'd never know what might await us below." Vinny swallowed hard. "We'd better keep quiet from here on," said Dermod, as he slowly began to descend the stone stairs. Vinny followed closely behind.

Cooley stood trembling with the hack-saw in his right hand and with his left hand gripping the silver band.

"Go on," insisted Doyler. "Cut it."

The hack-saw screeched as the teeth tore into the metal. He tore through it in a few seconds. The three men looked at each other, each afraid to make the next move, which would be to remove the coffin lid.

Dermod and Vinny had followed the light from the gas lamp and were quickly at the entrance to the vault. They pressed themselves to the walls on either side of the entrance and peered in from the shadows. They could see the three men standing beside an old marble tomb.

Doyler stood at the top of the black coffin lid and Cooley at the end. They stared at each other in nervous anticipation. "Here goes," said Doyler, trying to make light of the situation. They raised the lid only a few inches and, as they did so, they heard an horrific roar, like the sound of an angry lion. The lid shot out of their hands into the air and crashed to the floor. The coffin began to rock from side to side. Heavy grey smoke boiled out from it, instantly changing to a slime-green colour.

Doyler and Cooley screamed with fright and leapt into each other's arms. The doctor was physically shaken as he saw the green clouds form into the shape of a man.

Dermod and Vinny watched in absolute horror what was manifesting itself in front of their very eyes. Then the smoke cleared and, standing in the coffin before them, was a tall, gaunt, grotesque figure, with thin grey hair, sunken eyes and a skeletal face with stretched leathery-green skin. He extended his arm, raised his hand, and pointed a long, bony finger at the doctor. The overgrown nails had the appearance of talons. He demanded to know why they had come here.

"Who dares enter here?" the vampire hissed.

"We have not come to harm you, only to help!" The doctor stammered the words, then recovered a little to explain to this horrific-looking creature that his name was Doctor Drachler and that he had spent over forty years studying ancient cultures, trying to prove the existence of the supernatural. There was great excitement in his voice. "Tonight I have finally done it!"

The vampire snarled, showing his sharp fangs. "I have been locked up here for over a century because of a foolish priest and a stupid blacksmith. I should have destroyed them first." Then he smiled an evil grin. "It doesn't matter, now that I am set free again – they are mere dust by now. But I will exact revenge from their descendants. We vampires have a long memory." Then, staring at Doyler and Cooley, who were still clutching each other he demanded, "Who are these snivelling idiots? A food supply?"

"No, they are my assistants who helped me to release you. They have been very helpful and will be useful in the future."

"The thirst is upon me; I need sustenance," the vampire declared, staring at Doyler and Cooley.

"No, please," pleaded Doyler. "Spare us."

The vampire stepped out of the coffin and on to the ground. Eddies of dust puffed up as he moved towards the two men.

"Stop," said the doctor. The vampire turned around. There was rage in his face. "I have brought you some sustenance." The vampire stopped and looked puzzled. The doctor quickly hurried over to the wicker basket and lifted out a beautiful Siamese cat. He offered the cat to the vampire.

The vampire gently took it and stroked it. "Since I know your intentions are good, I will accept your gift and spare these two creatures."

"Thank you," blurted Doyler. "We're very grateful."

"Silence," commanded the vampire. "Before I change my mind." The cat hissed and became limp. Doyler and Cooley turned away from the sickening sight. "A little sustenance and my thirst has been slaked." The vampire spoke through bloodstained teeth. "But be warned," he continued. "I will not remain satisfied going through life feeding on mere cats and the like."

"This is the end of the twentieth century. Things are very different. You might find it a very interesting time to live in. I guarantee it will be different from any century you have ever known."

"How different?" asked the vampire, becoming interested.

Holding a handkerchief to his mouth, and trying not to retch from the foul breath of the vampire, who had moved closer to him, Doctor Drachler spoke. "I will explain all. If you let me assist you, I can make you famous. You can have an old castle, live in luxury, have servants."

"I once had all these things. I am from a very distinguished family of eastern Europe. I am Count Vedil."

"You can have all these again in the west, whether you choose America, Great Britain, France, Spain . . . the choice is yours."

"How this century has changed from other centuries – you would welcome one as myself, a vampire?"

"Everything is up for grabs this century. You could be the darling of the media. Be on radio and television."

"What is all this talk?" the vampire snapped.

The doctor continued excitedly. "They would write books and articles about you. People would travel great distances to visit you. Kings, queens, philosophers, scientists, priests, cardinals, ministers . . . all would want to meet you and discuss your life, your views, your philosophy. We could become rich and famous, we could become immortal!"

"I am already immortal," smiled the vampire, whose physical appearance had radically changed – the semblance of a handsome young man was appearing.

"There is one stipulation," said the doctor.

"You want to put restrictions on Count Vedil? Who has

lived over five hundred years?" The vampire almost spat the words.

The doctor began to shudder as the vampire took a step closer to him. "I will serve you well, supply your blood needs each day, but you must not harm or kill anyone, least of all make anyone a vampire," said the doctor.

The vampire ran his fingers down his tweed lapel. His hand was like a claw as it scraped along the doctor's jacket. "You intrigue me. You will supply me with fresh blood?"

"Yes," said the doctor.

"I tell you," said the vampire, "I am not interested in living only on animal blood."

"This will be human blood. You will even be able to choose the blood type you prefer."

The vampire laughed a demonic laugh. "This is certainly a very interesting century."

"I will have to buy it," said the doctor. "But that is not a problem."

"So people are prepared to sell this precious substance? How very curious. Does not your Bible say 'the blood is the life'?"

"Will you agree?" the doctor asked.

"Let me tell you, dear doctor, only very special people are chosen by vampires to become as them. Most of the time, humans are merely a source of sustenance. After all, we would not want every second person walking the streets to be a vampire. That would be too much competition." He gave a deep sigh. "I have slept for so very long. The vampires' sleep is not like human sleep, which is merely a rehearsal for death. Our sleep is like being chained to our tomb awaiting release by the power of night."

"All this is most interesting," said the doctor. "And that is why people would want to hear you speak. They would hang on your every word."

"Well, I shall agree, dear doctor, if you promise to provide me with all that I demand, including a castle . . . a mansion might suffice. First, I will require a great deal of blood so I can return to my former self."

"It may take a day or two, but after that you will receive a daily supply," said the doctor reassuringly.

"I'm beginning to like this century already," laughed the vampire.

"I wonder what's keeping them," said Amanda. "They've been gone for over half an hour. I don't know about the rest of you, but I'm not sitting around here all night."

"I'll go with you," said Julie.

"You and Peter mind the car," said Amanda to Gary, who had finally woken up.

Amanda found it difficult to walk over the rough terrain in her high-heeled shoes, so she removed them.

"This place is very spooky at night-time," Julie remarked.

"Yes," said Amanda. "Maybe I shouldn't have allowed Dermod to indulge my freaky brother in his crazy schemes."

"I'm a member of the club as well," Julie smiled.

Arriving at the abbey, Amanda climbed over the wall and walked out into the courtyard. There was no sign of life anywhere. "Where have they gone to? Dermod! Vinny!" Amanda called in a loud voice. The names echoed around the old abbey. "I hope they're not playing some trick on us. Tomorrow is my birthday; I wouldn't be surprised if that Vinny suggested some prank or other. Oh, he's done it before."

Vinny and Dermod quaked as they heard Amanda's voice and their names being called. "Please, don't come down here," Vinny whispered to himself.

A predatory look came over the vampire as he heard the young woman's voice.

"We'd better warn them and get out of here," whispered Dermod to Vinny. As they turned to leave, they were pounced on by the vampire. He had a grip so tight around their throats that they could barely breathe. The vampire was about to dispatch them when the doctor pleaded with him not to. He indicated to Doyler and Cooley to tie them up and gag them. Without hesitation, Doyler and Cooley tied a rope around the two of them, stuffed a rag inside their mouths and then tied a handkerchief around their faces.

"Dermod! Dermod!" Amanda called, as she descended the steps. She saw a light at the end of the tunnel. She began to feel real fear, but the light in the vault drew her towards it. Julie clutched her arm tightly. "If they spring out on us, I'll kill them," said Amanda, not realising the deadly creature that lurked in the vaults.

"Are you in there, Vinny?" Amanda called. There was an edge to her voice. "This is not funny, you know." She stepped on the wooden door that lay at the entrance to the vault. They could see the gas lamp glowing warmly and a coffin lid on the ground.

Julie shrieked and pointed at the skeleton on the ground.

"That's enough," said Amanda. "We're out of here. I'm taking the car and they can bloomin' well walk to Dublin for all I care," As they turned to leave, they saw Doyler and Cooley pressed against the wall trembling. Over to the right they could see the doctor, standing beside Dermod and Vinny, who were bound and gagged.

Before Amanda could utter another word, a strong arm pulled her back. Julie turned and screamed wildly at the creature that had Amanda in a vice-like grip. Amanda was too terrified to look around, but was overpowered by the smell of the vile breath from the creature.

"All here, I trust?" said the vampire. Smelling the chamomile fragrance from Amanda's hair, he turned her around to face him. She stifled her desire to scream. "What a delightful creature," said the vampire. "Well worth waking up to. Such a delicate neck, like a swan." He bent closer. "And a very subtle perfume, how charming. This is truly a prize worth keeping." Amanda's breathing became uneven with anxiety. As she watched from the corner of her eyes his lips slowly parted, revealing needle-sharp teeth.

"Wait!" pleaded the doctor. "You promised. No killing . . . we made a deal."

"My dear doctor, there is one thing I forgot to mention. The thrill of the kill. Like hounds hunting down a fox, the excitement . . . nothing can equal it."

"Please," Amanda pleaded.

"Oh, the quarry's plaintive plea," he grinned malevolently. "What is it, my precious one?"

"I would just ask you one favour." Her voice trembled. "Let them go and I'll stay with you. I promise."

"Spoken like a true heroine. I hope your boyfriend is impressed." He grinned at Dermod who, unknown to the others, was busy cutting through the rope that bound them.

The vampire ran his hand up along Amanda's back and grabbed her hair with painful force. Her head jerked back and her mouth opened wide. "You are not in any position to bargain, young lady. I hold all the cards."

"Not quite all!" yelled Dermod who, by now, had freed himself and pulled down the handkerchief. He lunged across and stabbed the vampire in the arm. The pain was enough to make him loosen his grip on Amanda and she pulled away.

The vampire snarled, pulled out the knife, snapping it like a twig. "Get him," he commanded the others. But they did not move. He raised up his arm to show the wound. "You fools," he shouted, as the wound began to heal itself almost instantly. Then he turned to Dermod with the eyes of a killer and slowly stalked him. "I shall take great pleasure in destroying your boyfriend."

Suddenly the vampire recoiled in horror. Standing in front of him was young Peter, holding a brass crucifix in both hands. The vampire moved back. Peter stepped closer and touched the vampire on the arm. On contact, the vampire's arm began to burn. He screamed in pain and, with his other hand, knocked Peter to the ground, making him lose his grip on the crucifix.

Julie immediately rushed over and picked it up. With arms extended she held it high, pointing it directly at the vampire. The vampire couldn't bear to look upon the cross and pleaded with Julie to put it down. With shaking hands, she continued to ward off the vampire.

"I will come for you some night while you are sleeping," he hissed at Julie. "That's a promise. You are all going to die a most horrible death, do you hear me!"

The doctor moved up behind the vampire and pulled him firmly around. "Take that, Count Vedil." With his right hand, the doctor punctured the vampire's chest with a wooden stake, driving it with all his might into the vampire's black heart. A shriek of evil came from the vampire, as he gripped the stake with both his hands, trying desperately to remove it. He writhed and twisted like a giant serpent, staggering to the doorway before collapsing to his knees, snarling and still writhing as he fell. Dermod took the cross and pushed it towards him. As he did so, the vampire began to disintegrate in front of their very eyes until all that remained was a skull and some bones.

They all stood in silence, trying to come to terms with what they had just witnessed.

Then Doyler broke the silence. "Well done, doctor. You spiked him good. We can all rest easy in our beds tonight."

"Too true," said Cooley.

"It's a pity in some ways," sighed the doctor. "We could have learned so much from him. If only he could have accepted the ideas I put to him. I had such plans . . ."

"Never mind, Doctor," said Doyler. "A creature like that could never be trusted. You know the old saying, a leopard can't change his spots."

"Maybe you're right. Well, so much for having proof that vampires existed," he sighed.

"Hold your horses," said Cooley. "Haven't you the journal? This skull here . . ." he picked it up and pointed to the fangs. "Not to mention the coffin. They'll all go to make a ghoulish exhibit somewhere."

"You're right," smiled the doctor. Then, turning to the others, he continued. "I recognise you three from the art gallery. Am I right?" Vinny, Julie and Peter nodded. "And, if I'm not mistaken, I saw you, young lady, in a public house with these two gentlemen?"

"Yes, only I wasn't really with them," Amanda smiled broadly. "Well, I think we should all leave," she suggested.

"I don't know what to say, except to apologise for putting your lives in danger because of an old man's obsession with the unknown," declared Doctor Drachler.

"You didn't force us to come here," said Amanda.

"I don't know whether this is an appropriate thing to suggest, but may I offer to buy you all supper on the way home to Dublin?"

Amanda looked at Dermod. "That would be a grand way to end the evening."

Then the doctor added solemnly, "I don't think we should tell a soul about what happened here tonight. I shudder to think what the tabloid newspapers would make of it. None of us would have any peace."

"I'm sure you're not collecting all these items for nothing," said Amanda.

"You're a clever girl, Amanda. All will be revealed in my own good time. Shall we go? And perhaps you could recommend a good restaurant?"

"I don't think we should have steaks," said Cooley, smiling weakly.

They all laughed loudly.

"Can we get chips?" asked Peter, which brought more laughter.

Doyler extended his hand to Dermod. "Sorry about that, I mean, tying you up. We didn't really mean to, we were sort of pressured . . . we're really squeaky-clean chaps."

Dermod eyed him suspiciously before offering him his hand.

They made their way out of the vault, along the tunnel, then up the stairs to the courtyard.

"Where's Gary?" asked Amanda, becoming anxious.

"He's really exhausted," said Peter. "When you got out of the car he went back to sleep."

"He's the sensible one," declared the doctor. Turning to Doyler and Cooley, he ordered, "Bring the coffin, the skull, and anything else you think I might need. I will pay you two handsomely." Then he left with the others.

"Well, at least we won't be out of pocket," grinned Doyler.

"Who would have imagined it?" said Cooley, looking about the vault. "A real, live vampire living here."

"A very dead one now, thank heavens," said Doyler, as he lifted up the lid of the coffin.

Doyler and Cooley carried the heavy coffin over the broken wall to their van.

"Stop at Arklow," suggested Doyler, as he and Cooley loaded the coffin into the van.

"See you later," said the others, as they hurried to their cars and sped away from the abbey.

"I hope the doors will close on the van with this coffin. We don't want a guard pulling us over and us trying to explain it."

"Push it up towards the passenger side on to the seat. See, it fits fine," said Cooley.

"What will you do?" asked Doyler. "Lie in the coffin from here to Dublin?"

"No way. I'll sit in the back beside it. By the way, what was in that brown cardboard box?" Cooley wondered.

"Well, it's there. I didn't leave anything of value behind," grinned Doyler.

Cooley opened it carefully. "Well, look at this. A dress suit and a black cloak, beautifully lined in red velvet. Must have been a present for the vampire from the doctor."

"We could sell it," said Doyler.

"No," said Cooley. "We'd better give it back to the doctor. It can be part of his exhibit." Doyler's expression suddenly changed and he appeared very anxious, scratching his stubble then his belly. Cooley picked up on his anxiety. "What's the matter?"

"Where's the skull?" asked Doyler.

"You brought it," insisted Cooley.

"No, I didn't. You'd better go back down for it."

"There's no way I'm ever going down there again. The place looked like it was about to collapse at any moment."

Doyler reached for a hessian sack and pulled out the skull. Cooley punched him in mock annoyance. "Alas, poor Yorick . . ." said Doyler. "You're worth more money this way."

"I reckon we could be talking about a new Hiace van for all our troubles; well, at least a '94 job," suggested Cooley.

"You're right," said Doyler. "And, you know something? I think we should make a small donation to the cat society as well." Cooley looked at him and grinned nervously. "You're giving me the shivers again."

"Let's go. I'm starving," said Doyler.

"You've the constitution of an ox, Doyler," quipped Cooley. "Nothing will put you off your grub."

"That's a fact," laughed Doyler as he started up the engine and pulled away.

# Chapter Eleven

"Happy Birthday, dear Amanda, Happy Birthday to you!"

"You shouldn't have gone to all this trouble," Amanda declared, kissing her mother warmly on her cheek.

Her dad produced a present from behind his back. "If you don't like it, I can change it," he added.

"Thanks, Da. I'm sure I'll love it," she reassured him, opening up the present. "A CD player! That's lovely." She hugged him, then turned to her brother. "You keep your hands off it."

Vinny smiled back. "Here's a present from me to you."

Amanda opened Vinny's gift. "A book! *Interview with the Vampire*!" She hit him lightly on the head with it.

There were two sharp rings of the doorbell. "It's for you, Amanda," said her dad. "Tony and Helen. They won't come in," he said in puzzled tones.

"Hi!" said Amanda, as she walked to the front door.

"Happy birthday!" They each had a small present for her. "It's your favourite perfume," said Helen. There was a slight awkwardness in her voice.

"Come on in," insisted Amanda.

"No, thanks," said Tony.

"What is it? You both look like cats that swallowed the prize canary."

They looked at each other sheepishly. "We wanted you to hear it from us. Oh, I feel so bad . . ."

"What?" said Amanda. "It can't be that bad."

"It is," said Tony. "And telling you on your birthday . . ."

"I'm really sorry, and we're such good friends and all," Helen added.

"You're not making sense," said Amanda, with her hands on her hips.

Helen glanced at Tony, then back to Amanda. "Tony and I are an item. I mean, we sort of got together last night . . . we realise we've a lot in common . . ."

"We didn't plan to . . . as you know, I was supposed to be working but I was asked to swop with Freddie Taylor; he wanted to take Wednesday night off. I called for you earlier but I was told you were gone to Wexford. What was on in Wexford?" asked Tony awkwardly.

"Ah . . . nothing . . ." said Amanda. "Listen, you two. It's all right. I don't really mind. It's not as if Tony and I were engaged and had put a deposit on a house, or something. It was only very casual with us."

"I thought it was more," said Tony, feeling a little hurt and surprised.

"You know what I mean, now. Come in and have a glass of champagne for my birthday. My dad goes over the top on my birthday, you know what he's like." Amanda showed them in and closed the hall-door behind her.

Almost immediately, there was another ring of the bell. "Who's a popular young lady today?" said her dad.

"It's probably someone for Vinny." Amanda opened the door. There stood Dermod with a large, beautifully-wrapped present and a bunch of red roses.

"Happy birthday!" he said softly. "How are you today after last night's adventure?"

"Just grand. I think I aged ten years," she smiled, grabbing him by his jacket collar and kissing him on the cheek, then ushering him into the sitting-room. "Have you met Dermod? He was the one who drove me to Wexford last night." Amanda held Dermod's hand and whispered warmly in his ear. "I expect you to write a best-seller after last night." Then she kissed him again.

Tony and Helen looked on in amazement, as did her mother and father. Vinny grinned and winked at Dermod.

# Chapter Twelve

Uncle Tommy arrived back from the shop on his bicycle with his groceries. He saw Vinny and his friends bikes around the side entrance to his house. He tiptoed over to the carriage and popped his head in.

"Good afternoon, everyone. Had a good day in school?"

"Yes, thanks," said Julie.

Then Uncle Tommy noticed that all the horror posters and film stills had been taken down. "What's up?" he enquired.

"We've decided not to have a horror club after all," said Vinny.

"That was a quick change of mind. The other day you were all keen," he remarked, then he saw the posters neatly packed on to the shelf. "I suppose you won't be needing the carriage." He looked disappointed.

"Oh, we will," said Julie.

"We thought we'd start an aliens club instead," Peter added.

"Like the *X-Files*," said Gary.

He rubbed his nose. "Mmm. Aliens? I must check. I know there were some great B-movies made in the early

'50s. Just let me think a minute. Listen, I'll just put on the kettle and butter up a few slices of batch loaf with cheese, and a few jam tarts and that will be the business. It'll give me time to remember what I have in the way of aliens films. Yes . . . there was that film *The Day The Earth Stood Still* . . ."

They watched him talking to himself as he crossed the lawn into the kitchen.

"My aunt's crucifix came in very handy on Saturday," said Peter.

"We said we were never going to mention it again," said Vinny anxiously. "I haven't slept properly since that night."

"I still get the creeps just thinking about it," said Julie.

"It sure was scary," said Peter.

"Of course, Gary had to sleep all the way through," said Vinny.

"It's not my fault I was tired. Anyway, it was me who came up with the idea for the aliens club," he said brightly.

"Just imagine . . ." said Peter. "Imagine we met a real alien."

"Don't start," said Julie.

"We're out for a walk one night," he continued. "Say, along Sandymount Strand. Suddenly, we see coloured lights in the night sky, high over the sea. We wonder is it a plane . . . then, at lightning speed, it shoots across the sky and stops over our heads. A door opens and out steps a green alien with a large bald head and slanted cat eyes. It points a finger at us. On the tip of the finger are suckers . . ."

The End